Nicky had to admit that it *felt* as if they were flying. The four-wheeler zoomed across the dark terrain so fast, there seemed to be no contact at all with the ground.

That was a problem. Especially when the tar pit below suddenly opened into what looked like an alien freeway—cram-packed with ground-flying transports.

"Nicky! Watch out!" Rachael cried, as they sped out into oncoming traffic.

Unfortunately, Rachael's screams came too late.

This time, Nicky Gogol really *was* going to crash.

DEADTIME STORIES™

Nightmare on Planet X

DEADTIME STORIES™

Nightmare on Planet X

A. G. Cascone

Troll

Copyright © 1997 by A. G. Cascone, Inc.

Published by Troll Communications L.L.C.

Deadtime Stories is a trademark of A. G. Cascone, Inc.

Printed in the United States of America.

10 9 8 7 6 5 4 3 2 1

For Anthony Bruno—
a good friend
on a strange and sometimes
terrifying planet

CHAPTER 1

When Nicky Gogol finally opened his eyes, he had no idea where he was. He was groggy and weak, and totally disoriented. Every inch of his body felt heavy. His head was throbbing.

"Mom?"

Nicky tried to call out to his mother. But his tongue felt swollen, as if it were wrapped up in cotton. His mouth was so dry, he could barely even swallow, much less speak.

Where am I? Nicky wondered nervously.

He tried to lift his head, but that was a big mistake.

Dangling directly above Nicky's face was a blinding white light. The beam of the light was so hot and so bright, Nicky thought it was going to burn holes through his eyeballs.

Nicky jerked his head back.

That was a bigger mistake.

Nicky's skull crashed down onto the cold metal slab beneath him, sending a sharp pain to his brain.

"*Ooooooooo-uch!*" Nicky's cries echoed through his head as an eerie sound reverberated through the room.

Be-beep, be-beep, be-beep . . .

It sounded like a radar bleep. But it was high-pitched and haunting.

The sound bounced off the cold, sterile walls, piercing Nicky's eardrums like daggers. He tried to cover his ears, but he couldn't lift his arms. Then he tried to sit up, but his waist wouldn't bend. And his legs wouldn't budge.

What the heck is going on?

Turning his head and looking out of the corner of his eye, Nicky could see below him dozens of strange wires snaking across the floor. Each one seemed to lead to the monitor of a giant computer. But it wasn't a normal-looking computer. It was a big black box that hung from a long silver pole.

The front of it was covered with knobs and flashing green lights. Above the knobs, the snakelike wires were plugged into tiny round sockets. The box was shaking and beeping like crazy . . . until Nicky glanced down at his chest.

Then the beeping suddenly stopped—along with Nicky's heart.

The wires weren't just plugged into the computer! They were attached to Nicky's chest with dozens of little round rubbery things that seemed to be sucking his skin off!

Panic immediately set in, jump-starting Nicky's heart.

The machine beeped wildly again.

"Somebody help me!" Nicky's voice finally burst through his dry, cracked lips.

Nicky tried to bolt upright, but his body wasn't just heavy—it was pinned to the metal slab he was lying on. Huge leather straps around his arms and his legs held Nicky in place. They were so tight, they were starting to cut off his circulation.

Nicky could hardly catch his breath.

As it was, the air in the room was unlike any air Nicky had ever filled his lungs with before. It was thick and musty. Nicky could actually see strange little particles flying through it.

Calm down! Nicky ordered himself, taking one slow breath after the other. *It's silly to panic.* At least that's what Nicky's dad always said when *he* was in scary situations. *There has to be a logical explanation for this.*

But what?

Nicky racked his brain trying to remember where he was and how he had gotten there. But his head was still in a fog. It took him forever just to remember what day it was—or at least what day he *thought* it was.

It's Friday, Nicky told himself. *Mom and Dad and Zoe and I were flying out to see Grandma this morning . . .*

Just then, terror tore through Nicky's heart like a laser as he remembered the horrible thing that had happened.

Oh my gosh! Nicky cried silently. *Our plane went down. We crashed! I must be in the hospital.*

But Nicky was only half right.

CHAPTER 2

Nicky's heart raced.

The machine bleeped in sync.

Wait a minute. Nicky was beginning to realize that something wasn't quite right. *If I am in the hospital, where're my mom and dad? Where's Zoe?*

Ordinarily, Nicky would have been grateful that Zoe wasn't around. In fact, he considered Zoe a screaming, moaning, miserable mutant—who just happened to be his younger sister. But the thought that something terrible might have happened to her actually had Nicky worried.

What if I'm all alone? Nicky wondered. *What if the rest of my family didn't survive the crash?*

No! Nicky quickly forced the idea from his head. *That can't be possible. Think,* he ordered himself. *Try to remember exactly what happened.*

Slowly, the fog in Nicky's brain started to clear. He remembered waking up in the morning . . . and fighting with Zoe over just about everything—including the fact that she had devoured the last of the Cocoa Comets, right before she'd ruined his Star Blaster, Nicky's favorite toy gun. They'd even had a fight over suitcases.

Luckily, Nicky won that battle. Even his mom understood that there was no way in the universe he could carry a pink princess suitcase. Especially not in front of all the guys who worked at Warpside Airport, where Nicky's dad kept his plane.

Nicky's dad was a licensed pilot. He'd even flown with the armed forces. In fact, Mr. Gogol had several aircraft of his own. He used the bigger planes for his import/export business. But the small craft he used for travel, mostly for short trips, such as the one they were taking to Grandma's house.

Flying to Grandma's house was always easier than driving, especially with Zoe in the car. Even in the Land Rover, driving to Grandma's house took like three thousand hours. And two thousand, nine hundred and ninety-nine of them were spent listening to Zoe whine, moan, and scream.

Zoe whined, moaned, and screamed in the plane, too, but at least it didn't last for eons.

In fact, Nicky was beginning to remember the screaming Zoe had been doing ten minutes after takeoff. She'd thrown a tizzy fit because Nicky's dad had let Nicky work the controls.

Mr. Gogol had been teaching Nicky how to fly for months, but so far they'd practiced only on the ground. On the way to Grandma's Mr. Gogol had finally agreed to let Nicky try out what he'd learned in the air. They'd been flying over what looked like a forest when Nicky's dad had handed over control of the altitude stick.

Nicky remembered feeling *soooooo* cool and so in control. He'd kept the plane steady and well above the treetops. The flying had been easy. There was hardly any turbulence, and not a cloud in the sky.

But something went terribly wrong.

All at once, the aircraft began to shake violently. It was so bad, Zoe's sirenlike scream sounded more like the trill of an opera singer.

The reading on the altitude meter started to plunge. So did the aircraft.

Nicky clutched the stick with both hands, frantically trying to pull up. But the stick wouldn't budge.

Suddenly an enormous shadow darkened the cockpit. Through the windshield, Nicky saw something huge looming over them. It was an aircraft, but it was unlike any aircraft Nicky had ever seen before.

Red, blinking lights swirled around the craft's metallic gray belly, while laserlike lights shot out from its nose.

Whatever it was, it seemed to be forcing their plane to descend.

The treetops were getting closer and closer. Within seconds, Nicky could hear them whipping the underside of their plane.

"We're going to crash!" Zoe's screams echoed through Nicky's head.

"Tighten your seat belts, everyone!" Mr. Gogol instructed as he tried to regain control.

Just then, the plane took a nosedive. Timber splintered against sheet metal as the plane plunged into the forest. A deafening *riiiiiiiiip* filled the air as both wings were torn from the plane.

Within seconds, they were plummeting toward the earth with the speed of a rocket.

But just as it was about to hit the ground, the plane jerked to a halt. It was as if a giant hand had grabbed it by its tail in midair. There they were, frozen in a nosedive, less than fifty feet from disaster.

Nicky thought it was some kind of miracle. Until the plane started to ascend again—without any wings.

It wasn't a miracle. The frightening aircraft was back! Only this time, it wasn't forcing their plane down. It was sucking it up to its enormous gray belly.

A long, thick cable hung from an open flap in the center of that belly. At the end of the cable was a huge metal disk. The disk was stuck to the top of their plane, and it seemed to be acting as a magnet.

Higher and higher they went, dangling from the end of the line like a bunch of dead fish. The strange craft was reeling them in and swallowing them whole!

Inside the beast, Nicky couldn't see anything but blackness. He remembered a strange white mist pouring through the cracks of their plane and burning his nostrils.

And then he had felt his entire body going limp.

That was the last thing Nicky could remember.

For a moment, he felt relieved. *You see?* he told himself. *No one was hurt in the crash. That giant thing saved us!*

But as Nicky looked back down at the wires running from his chest, his relief faded fast.

What the heck was that giant aircraft? he wondered. *And where the heck am I now?*

Nicky struggled to free himself from the straps. He wanted to get out of there. He wanted to find his parents. He even wanted to find Zoe. More than anything, he just wanted to go home!

The machine beeped wildly again.

"Help!" Nicky called out, pulling against the straps to no avail. "Somebody help me!"

Behind the glare of light above, Nicky could see three separate figures moving toward him.

"Mom?" Nicky called out nervously. "Dad? Is that you?"

There was no response.

"Zoe?" Nicky tried again.

But still there was silence.

"Who's there?" Nicky wanted to know . . . until he saw three freaky creatures stepping out of the shadows.

Aliens! Nicky's brain screamed as the truth finally dawned on him. *We've been abducted by aliens!*

CHAPTER 3

Nicky was terrified. Everything started to spin.

The three creatures looming over him were more hideous than anything he could have imagined. They were more grotesque than any alien Nicky had ever seen on film, or in any of his science fiction books.

Their heads were big, totally out of proportion to their freaky long bodies. And their gross squished-up faces were *way* out of proportion to their disgusting fat heads! Their dark rounded eyes were creepy enough. But the size of their noses made Nicky want to throw up.

At least, Nicky thought they were noses, but who could be sure?

Still, one thing was certain. Nicky had no desire to find out what kind of alien stuff dripped out of *those* tunnel-like holes.

Their skin was putrid and pale, and covered with pockmarks and bumps. One of the aliens, the biggest of the three, had short, wiry black strings shooting out of his arms. He reached out to touch Nicky.

Nicky let out a blood-curdling scream.

"Aaaaaaaaaaggghh!" he cried. "Leave me alone!"

The sound of Nicky's scream bounced off the walls. The aliens covered their strange-looking ears as if they were in pain.

When Nicky ran out of breath, the big alien started to ramble in some kind of gibberish. Nicky tried to understand what he was saying. But the deep sounds coming from the alien's blubbery lips were stranger than any foreign language Nicky had ever heard. Still, Nicky could tell that the big alien was the leader. The other two creatures suddenly scurried around, obeying his orders.

The medium-sized one raced to the black box and twisted a blue knob. The stubby-looking one ran to the corner of the room and turned on yet another *bleeping* machine. This one drew lines on a screen, green, squiggly lines that climbed up and down like the peaks of a mountain.

Just then, the big alien reached out to touch Nicky again. Nicky wanted to scream. But the moment he felt the long, icy fingers wrap around his wrist, something strange began to happen. It was as if the alien's touch was sending some kind of signal to Nicky's brain, a signal that seemed to open a new door inside Nicky's head.

Oh my gosh, Nicky thought. Suddenly, he could understand every word the aliens were saying.

"The pulse is very, very strong," the big alien was telling the others. "He's coming around quite nicely."

Holy smokes, Nicky thought. *Maybe I'm in some kind of alien hospital.*

"Do you want me to prepare the surgical tools?" one of the other aliens asked.

Surgical tools? Nicky gulped. What did they need surgical tools for? He was feeling just fine.

As Nicky got more upset, the mountain machine practically drew Mt. Everest.

The big alien frowned at the machine.

"Not yet," he answered. "I want to make sure his condition is stable before we begin."

Begin what? Nicky wondered nervously.

"What about the others, Dr. Ickle?" the smallest alien suddenly asked.

Dr. Ickle? What kind of a name is that?

If Nicky hadn't been so terrified, he might have laughed. But Nicky *was* terrified. Especially since he was pretty sure that the little alien was talking about his family.

"I haven't decided what to do with the other alien creatures yet," Dr. Ickle answered.

Alien creatures? Nicky couldn't believe what he was hearing. *Is this guy out of his mind? We're not the aliens—they are!*

"Hey!" Nicky blurted out in his own language. "We're not alien creatures! We're an intelligent life form!"

Nicky was hoping the aliens would be able to understand *him* the way *he* understood *them*. But Dr. Ickle just stared at him curiously, as if he were some kind of fascinating specimen.

The medium-sized alien quickly backed away. "Be careful!" the alien warned. "I think the creature is getting angry."

"I'm not a creature!" Nicky shouted again.

"Don't worry about our little friend," Dr. Ickle said. He came closer and stroked Nicky's head with his long, icy fingers. "He's tightly secured. He can't possibly hurt us."

"But what if he's got special powers?" the little one asked nervously. "What if he can kill with his eyes?"

"Don't be ridiculous." Dr. Ickle laughed. "If any one of these aliens could have killed us with special powers, it would have happened already."

"I still think we should be careful," the little one said.

Nicky was nervous too. He had to find a way to get these creeps to leave him alone. Maybe he could communicate in *their* language. Maybe that would work.

Nicky twisted his lips, struggling to pronounce the alien words. "WE ARE NOT ALIEN CREATURES!" he said slowly, surprised at the strange sounds coming out of his mouth.

Nicky had obviously said something correctly. The aliens were all staring at him with startled expressions.

"My, my, my." Dr. Ickle's puffed lips twisted upward into a grin. "You are a clever little fellow, aren't you? Look at that," he went on. "You haven't been here a week and already you're learning our language."

A week! Nicky was shocked. That much time had gone by?

"You're so very, very clever," Ickle continued. "I can't wait to study your brain!" He rubbed his icky hands together. "I'm going to learn a lot from you, aren't I?"

Whew! Nicky thought, relief flooding over him. *This guy just wants me to teach him stuff. That's cool. I can handle that.*

But Nicky was wrong. He knew it the moment Ickle reached into the pocket of his weird floppy coat and pulled out a razor-sharp blade.

Dr. Ickle was going to pick Nicky's brain all right—after he removed it from Nicky's head!

CHAPTER

4

Nicky's flesh crawled as Dr. Ickle came closer with his sharp instrument.

"Nooooooo!" Nicky cried. He felt like a roast about to be carved for a feast. "Don't cut me up!"

Nicky was so terrified, he wasn't speaking the aliens' language anymore; he was speaking his own. And Dr. Ickle didn't understand a word of it.

"Don't be frightened," Ickle said, sizing up Nicky's skull. "I'm just trying to get to know you—piece by bloody piece." He let out a horrible honk that started in his bloated stomach and shot straight through his nose.

"Let me out of here!" Nicky screamed, struggling against the straps.

"You know," Ickle informed him, "you shouldn't be squiggling so much. You're only going to make things more difficult for yourself, and messy for me. If you'd just lie still, your brain will be out in a moment. And trust me, after that you won't feel a thing."

Suddenly, a swirling red light spun through the room.

"Uh-oh," the littlest alien said. "There must be a problem with one of the other specimens."

"I bet it's that tiny female mutant," the medium-sized alien chimed in. "That creature is getting on everyone's nerves."

Now Nicky was sure they were talking about Zoe. Leave it to his little sister to get on the aliens' nerves too.

"Darn," Dr. Ickle huffed, tossing his blade into the small metal tray sitting on the table next to Nicky's slab. "I guess we'd better check on the little beast before she gives everyone in Research a migraine."

"Maybe you ought to cut *her* organs out, Dr. Ickle," the littlest alien suggested. "Starting with her vocal cords."

Nicky gulped. Under any other circumstances, the idea of Zoe's being silent for the rest of her life would be appealing. But the thought of an alien ripping her throat out was horrifying.

Luckily, Dr. Ickle's response calmed Nicky's fears.

"No," he said. "We'll save the littlest one for the zoo. She is, after all, the most savage of the four. I don't want a single hair on her head touched. Understood?"

The other aliens nodded. But they didn't look happy.

"We'll just have to figure out a way to keep her mouth sealed while she's in here," Ickle added. Then he glanced back at Nicky. "You, my friend, are going to have to wait while we check on the screaming me-me. Besides, I need more tools before we begin. Relax. We'll be back in a flash."

With that, Ickle and his sidekicks disappeared.

"Her name is Zoe!" Nicky called after them. "Not screaming me-me!"

The only reply was the sound of a door clanging shut.

Oh, man, Nicky thought desperately. *I have to get out of here. I have to get to Zoe—and find Mom and Dad.*

Just then, a shiny object caught his eye—it was the blade of Ickle's knife.

Nicky's heart skipped a beat. *If I can get to that knife, I bet I can cut through these straps,* he thought.

But how? Nicky lay flat on his back, with his arms strapped down.

Maybe I can lean over and stretch out my neck, he thought. Then he could pick up the blade with his teeth.

But Nicky quickly realized that that wasn't going to work. Even Rubber Man from his comic books couldn't stretch that far.

Just then, the door clanged open again. An icy chill went through Nicky as footsteps approached. Ickle was back with his torture tools.

But it wasn't Dr. Ickle. It wasn't any of the aliens Nicky had met.

The alien who'd entered the room was tiny, much smaller than the others, and not nearly as ugly. Its eyes weren't round, dark, and cold. They were oval and blue, and they shone like crystals. Dangling below its ear-holes were two clumps of silver, almost like earrings. And draped across its neck were tiny clusters of gold linked in strange little balls.

Nicky was pretty sure that this was a young female alien. She had the same black wiry stuff as Ickle shooting out of her. But it was coming not out of her arms but out of her head. And it was tied in a knot with a shiny blue string.

For a moment, the little alien just stood there, staring into Nicky's eyes. "You poor little guy," she whispered. "How could they do this to you? How?"

Nicky didn't answer. He just stared back at her.

"Ooooooooh," the alien girl huffed, stomping her stubby feet. A gooey liquid oozed from her eyes, then down her puffed cheeks. "I hate my Uncle Ickle for this! I hate him!"

It took Nicky a minute to understand the alien word for "uncle."

"Uncle Ickle didn't hurt you, did he?" she asked.

Still Nicky stayed silent, trying to decide whether to trust this new alien.

"Well, I'm not going to let him and his scientist friends touch you," she went on, patting Nicky's hand. "Uncle Ickle thinks he's so great." Her voice started to change. "But he *isn't* great. He's a jerk! No! He's worse than a jerk. He's a cold-blooded iceman. Ickle the Iceman! And I'm going to fix him but good!"

Nicky wanted to believe that this was a friendly alien. But she was beginning to sound pretty hostile. And why should he trust any one of them when Ickle was planning to cut him to pieces and put his sister in a zoo?

And what about his parents? What were they going to do with them?

That thought alone made Nicky wince.

The alien girl noticed. "I'm sorry," she said more softly. "I scared you, didn't I?"

Nicky stayed silent.

"You probably don't even understand what I'm saying, do you? My name is Rachael." She introduced herself as if Nicky were an idiot. "Ra-chael." She repeated each syllable slowly.

Nicky still didn't speak.

"I don't have any parents, you know," she continued, eyeing Ickle's knife. "That's why I have to live with Ickle the Iceman. I'd much rather live with my grandmother."

Nicky watched nervously as "Ra-chael" picked up the knife.

"But," she went on, more to herself than to Nicky, "no one will let me live with my grandmother because the Zoning Board hasn't planned any schools up there yet. And nobody wants to deal with the transportation. But I don't care about school. I'd rather be lost out in space than spend another moment with Ickle."

Nicky felt a slight flicker of hope. This girl was an alien, but they had things in common. They both couldn't stand school, and they both had grandmothers who lived in the middle of nowhere, grandmothers whom they loved.

But the flicker of hope faded fast when Rachael

suddenly turned the tip of the blade toward Nicky's chest.

"I've run away a dozen times, you know," she informed him. "But this time, I'm running so far that no one will ever find me, not in a million years. And I'm going to make sure they don't find you either."

What the heck is she talking about? Nicky started to sweat. *And what's she planning to do with that knife?*

Slowly, she lowered the blade to his flesh. The lines on the monitor began to rise as Nicky started to panic.

"Uncle Ickle thinks he's the best scientist on the planet," Rachael went on. She laughed loudly. "But I'm going to get even with him. When he comes back to examine his little alien specimen . . ." As she leaned over Nicky, the blade glinted in the room's harsh light.

Desperately, he strained to get away.

Rachael, the little alien girl, was going to get even all right. She was planning to cut Nicky's heart out—before Ickle could get to his brain!

CHAPTER 5

Nicky closed his eyes as Rachael started sawing away with Ickle's sharp knife. *Please don't let it hurt,* he thought. He braced himself to feel a searing hot pain as the knife sliced through his chest.

But to Nicky's surprise, he didn't feel a thing.

His eyes shot open. Rachael wasn't trying to cut out his heart. She was trying to cut off the straps!

"I hope you understand what I'm saying," Rachael murmured as she sawed through the strap on his wrist. "I'm trying to help you escape. I'm trying to help you get to your family."

She's got to be kidding me, Nicky thought. *Why would an alien want to do that?*

"Once you're free, *you* have to help *me,*" Rachael went on. "I want you to take me back to your planet so that Ickle never finds me."

Abruptly, Rachael stopped sawing and glared at Nicky. "So? Do we have a deal or not?"

Nicky hesitated. She was only halfway through the strap—not nearly enough for Nicky to pull free.

What if it's some kind of trap? he thought. Maybe Rachael was just trying to get information for Ickle. Maybe Ickle and the aliens were planning to take over Nicky's planet.

"Well?" Rachael demanded.

Nicky stayed silent for a moment as he studied Rachael's face. While he certainly wasn't an expert on alien expressions, Rachael did have friendly eyes. And she sounded sincere. Maybe she really *was* trying to help him escape.

"Look," Rachael huffed. "I know you can talk. I heard my uncle telling the other scientists that you speak some kind of gobbledygook. So say something to me. Tell me we've got a deal."

One thing was clear. If Nicky didn't do something fast, Rachael would stop cutting the straps. Then Nicky would have no hope of escaping.

Nicky nervously cleared his throat. Then he tried to imitate her language as best as he could. "Okay," he blurted out. "It's a deal."

"You *can* speak!" Rachael squealed, showing two rows of jagged white rocks in her mouth. "And you speak in our language!"

Nicky smiled.

"This is too cool!" she went on. "But there's no time for

us to be chitchatting now. We have to get you out of here before Uncle Ickle comes back."

Nicky watched as Rachael started sawing more furiously than ever. She cut the straps in no time at all. Then she pulled the wires from Nicky's chest and helped Nicky to his feet.

"Now, you have to stay quiet," she said, dragging Nicky by the hand as though he were a child. "Otherwise you'll set off the hallway alarms. And don't let go of my hand," she instructed. "You have to stay close."

As if Nicky had a choice—Rachael's grip was viselike. No doubt about it, alien girls were just as strong as the girls on his planet.

The moment they'd crossed the room and stepped through the clanging door, Rachael spun her neck around like some kind of periscope.

"Okay," she said. "The coast is clear. Just keep your fingers crossed that it stays that way."

Yeah, right, Nicky thought. *Like that's going to help.*

"You can do that, can't you?" Rachael asked. "Cross your fingers, I mean."

Nicky shot her a look. How stupid did these aliens think he was?

Of course I can do that! Nicky wanted to shout. But he was afraid to set off the "hallway alarm." So he stuck out his hand and crossed his two digits.

Rachael looked truly impressed. "You really are an intelligent life form, aren't you?"

Uh-duuuhhhhh! Nicky wanted to shoot back.

Luckily, Rachael ran out of time for more "stupid-alien tricks." Just then, a ringing sound shook the walls.

"Uh-oh," Rachael said. "We'd better move it, before everyone starts heading to Level Three. That's where the cafeteria is."

Rachael took off. Nicky found himself flying like a flag at the end of an alien arm-pole.

Not only were alien girls strong, they were faster than lightning!

As Rachael raced through the tunnel, Nicky's feet barely touched down.

"Your parents are right down there," she said, pointing with her long skinny finger. "They're in Lab Number Six."

They started toward Lab Six. The problem was, they were about to ram into a solid wall.

It wasn't *really* a wall. It was the biggest, meanest-looking alien Nicky had seen yet. And the alien was standing next to another creepy creature that looked like a beanpole.

They were positioned in front of the door to Lab Number Six. And they were both holding what looked like ray guns.

Rachael stopped short. But the sight of the ray guns made Nicky gasp.

Suddenly, the "alien-in-the-hallway alarm" went off. Before Nicky could even try to make a move, the ray guns were pointed right at his face.

"Halt!" the boulder commanded. "Don't move a muscle, or I'll shoot!"

CHAPTER 6

Nicky's knees were knocking like crazy. He couldn't imagine what kind of killer death rays might come flying out of the strange-looking weapons pointed at him.

Maybe they were lasers that would turn him into a puddle of goo!

Nicky tried to look past the weapons, into the eyes of the creatures behind them.

If he could just communicate with them . . . maybe he could convince them not to shoot.

But the expressions chiseled onto the faces of these alien thugs were harder than stone. They looked like a couple of killing machines, made of putrid, gross flesh. The one built like a boulder had the fattest neck Nicky had ever seen. It was so fat, he could probably swallow a twelve-year-old whole. A twelve-year-old, just like Nicky!

Nicky's brain was screaming even louder than the "alien-in-the-hallway alarm." *Oh, man! What if Fat Neck really does try to eat me?*

Nicky had to do something before the skinny alien started to shoot or Fat Neck started to chew.

Nicky tried to speak, but what came out was a frightened croak.

Fat Neck and Skinny stepped forward.

"Wait!" Nicky forced another sound from his throat. "I come in peace!" he blurted out. It was the first thing he could think of.

It was a line Nicky had read in *Alien Androids,* one of his favorite comic books. It had worked in the comic book, when Jonah Brightstar, the superhero, encountered one of the fierce androids.

But it didn't work with Fat Neck and Skinny. On the contrary, they took another step closer, aiming to fire.

"Stop!" Rachael shouted, jumping in front of Nicky. "If you want to shoot him, you'll have to shoot me first!"

Nicky couldn't believe what Rachael was doing. She was going to get killed!

Skinny lowered his weapon, then gave Fat Neck a shove. "Don't fire!" he shouted. "That's Dr. Ickle's niece!"

It took a few seconds for the news to penetrate Fat Neck's fat head, but he finally lowered his gun.

"Move away from the alien, Rachael," Skinny demanded. "He's a dangerous creature."

Nicky resented that. First of all, he wasn't an alien. And if Skinny wanted to see a dangerous creature, all he had to do was take a look at Fat Neck—and himself!

Rachael stayed right where she was, shielding Nicky with her body. "When I say go," she whispered over her shoulder, "start running!"

Rachael began backing up, with Nicky behind her.

"Halt!" Fat Neck ordered, leveling his weapon.

"Didn't you hear me?" Skinny snarled at Fat Neck. "That's Dr. Ickle's niece. If we hurt her, Ickle will eat our hearts out."

"Yeah, but if we let that alien get away, Ickle will ice us for sure," Fat Neck shot back.

As the two alien goons argued, Rachael spun Nicky around and gave him a shove.

"Go!" she yelled, pushing him hard.

As Nicky started to run, Rachael took off after him.

"Halt!" Fat Neck shouted.

Nicky and Rachael kept running.

"Stop or I'll shoot," Fat Neck threatened again.

"Just keep going," Rachael insisted. "He won't shoot as long as I'm in the way."

At the end of the tunnel, Rachael grabbed Nicky's arm and pulled him through another steel door.

This one opened into what looked like a bottomless pit. There was nothing but darkness, and nowhere to go but down.

"Move it," Rachael said, pushing Nicky onto the ledge.

Are you nuts? Nicky wanted to ask. But he couldn't translate the words fast enough.

"This is a stairwell," she told Nicky, pointing downward.

"And those are the stairs. You're not going to fall. I promise."

Nicky looked down. In the darkness, he could make out dozens of strange-looking platforms suspended below. They didn't seem very sturdy, but when Rachael gave him a shove, he had no choice but to take the first step.

To his relief, the platform beneath his feet didn't collapse. And once Nicky got the hang of it, he and Rachael began running down the rest of the "stairs" even faster.

When they got to the bottom of the pit, another door awaited. Nicky pushed it open and peered inside. The room was filled with aliens dressed in outfits that looked like pajamas.

"This is the psycho ward," Rachael whispered to Nicky. "Don't worry. No one will even notice us down here. They're all nuts."

Unlike everybody else I've met so far, Nicky thought.

Just as Rachael and Nicky took off through the ward, Fat Neck and Skinny burst through the door.

"Stop them, you noo-noos!" Fat Neck hollered at the aliens in pajamas. "Don't let those two get away!"

The aliens on the psycho ward may have been nuts, but they were definitely sane enough to notice that Nicky just didn't blend. As he and Rachael tried to get lost in the crowd, some of the "noo-noos" started to chitchat about outer space, while others began to scream.

"Darn it!" Rachael cried. "Now what are we doing to do?"

Like Nicky had an answer.

"Wait a minute." Rachael had an idea. "We can hide in

the basement. Nobody ever goes down there anymore. They used to use it for storage, but they stopped because nobody wanted to travel that far for supplies."

Where the heck is the basement? Nicky wondered. *On the moon?*

"Come on," Rachael said, pulling him along. "This will be perfect. No one will even hear us down there. It's totally soundproof."

Within seconds, Nicky was flying like a flag behind Rachael again. They left Fat Neck and Skinny in the dust.

The trip to the basement took nowhere near as long as a trip to the moon. In fact, it took only a few seconds.

As soon as they entered the room, Nicky knew why nobody went down there. The basement was the coldest, dankest place Nicky had ever seen.

Long, elastic-like strings dangled from the ceiling. The only light came from a tiny blob of glass in the center of the ceiling. The light was yellow and dim, and it cast weird shadows.

Nicky swallowed hard. Suddenly, the psycho ward was looking a lot better.

"I'm telling you," Rachael said as if she could read his mind, "we're going to be fine down here." She opened a dusty, cracked door. "We can hide in this room until it's safe to come out."

But it wasn't even safe to go in!

Because there, on the other side of the door, was the cruelest creature of all.

CHAPTER 7

Nicky's heart dropped down to his stomach. Beside him, Rachael made a startled sound.

In the middle of the room was a cold metal slab, just like the one Nicky had been strapped to. But tied to this slab was Zoe, Nicky's five-year-old sister.

She was trying to scream. But her mouth was covered with a cellophane-like material that locked her lips together.

For once, though, Zoe wasn't the most frightening sight in the room. Looming over her was Ickle the Iceman!

Dr. Ickle held a long silver spike aimed at Zoe's eye. At the end of it was a giant plastic container filled with red liquid. It looked like some kind of injection device.

Ickle's about to ice Zoe, Nicky realized. He had to stop him!

Dr. Ickle spun around as Nicky and Rachael entered the room. Anger flashed in his eyes. "Stay right where you are," he growled. "Make one move and you'll be sorry."

Ickle was looking directly at Nicky. But his huge needle was still pointed at Zoe's eye.

Zoe was thrashing about wildly, trying to scream.

Just then, Nicky realized why Zoe was in the basement and not in a lab room. The basement was soundproof—at least that's what Rachael had said. Maybe the aliens had already figured out how bad Zoe's screaming could be. When Zoe exploded, it was like a tornado, leaving nothing but destruction in its path. Destruction and migraines.

Too bad her lips are sealed, Nicky thought. *One shriek from Zoe and Ickle would drop the needle and run.*

Nicky froze as Ickle stared at him. If he tried to make a move, Ickle was sure to stick *him* with the spike. Then there would be no way to save Zoe.

"'ick-y!" Zoe cried through the seal on her lips. "'elp me . . . or I'm 'elling 'ommy on you!"

Nicky couldn't believe it. Here they were, being held captive on an alien planet with a mad alien doctor about to spike Zoe's eyeball, and all Zoe could think about was tattling on Nicky.

Ickle spun toward Rachael. "What do you think you're doing with this alien?" he snapped.

"I'm trying to help him," Rachael shot back. "What you're doing is evil!"

"How dare you speak to me like that!" Ickle growled. "I deserve more respect from you, young lady," he told her.

"After all, I give you everything your bleeding heart desires. I even send you to the best school in the zone!"

"The Vroom School is a prison camp!" Rachael shouted. "I hate the Vroom School—almost as much as I HATE YOU!"

"I know you hate me," Ickle sneered. "But try to be reasonable. What I'm doing with these creatures is in the interest of science. Try to understand what an important discovery this is."

"You're a liar!" Rachael screamed at her uncle. "If you really cared about the 'interest of science,' you wouldn't be trying to hurt anyone. You'd be trying to convince the whole universe that even aliens have hearts and souls and feelings like we do!"

Nicky decided Rachael was pretty smart, at least for an alien.

Ickle didn't think so.

"You're such a silly girl, Rachael," he scoffed. "How can you say these creatures are just like us? Look at them. They're beastly."

If Nicky weren't trying to save his "alien" butt, he would have punched Ickle right in the nose.

"Ooooooohhhhh!" Rachael huffed, stomping her stubby feet. "There's no use talking to you. You'll never understand! Never!"

Rachael marched to the corner of the room. She picked up a long pole with loopy green hair on one end. Before Ickle could react, she rammed him right in the chest, pushing him to the ground.

In a flash, Rachael dropped the hairy pole. She rushed

over to Zoe and pulled the strange stuff from her lips.

"Wait!" Nicky warned. "Maybe you shouldn't—"

But it was too late. Zoe's earsplitting wail was already spinning through the place like a twister. And even though Rachael had said the place was soundproof, Nicky was sure the entire alien nation would be storming the basement at any moment.

Before Nicky could slap a hand over his sister's mouth, Ickle was back on his feet, headed for Nicky with the spike in his hand.

Nicky lunged for the hairy pole that Rachael had used. As Ickle approached, he swung it wildly, trying to keep the alien at bay.

"Come on, you stupid thing," Nicky shouted at the weapon in his hands. "Shoot a death ray or something!"

"That's not a weapon, you idiot," Dr. Ickle snarled as he dodged Nicky's advances. "That's a *mop*! You use it to wipe up the floor."

"Not where I come from, it isn't," Nicky shouted back.

While Nicky argued with Ickle, Rachael quickly untied Zoe.

For a moment, it looked as if they might actually escape. And then, sure enough, Zoe's screams brought in the reserves.

While it wasn't an *entire* alien nation that stormed the basement, it *was* Fat Neck and Skinny, with a bunch of their pals.

They were all carrying weapons. And they were *all* pointed at Nicky.

CHAPTER

8

Zoe stopped screaming when the platoon of aliens arrived.

"Freeze, you freaky little sucker," Fat Neck bellowed at Nicky. "Drop that mop before someone gets hurt!"

Nicky shook the "mop" at Fat Neck as hard as he could. But nothing happened.

"Be careful!" Rachael shouted. As Nicky turned to look at her, he saw Ickle pointing the spike at her.

"This is your last chance," Fat Neck warned. "Drop the mop or I shoot!" This time, Fat Neck pulled back the safety clip.

Nicky quickly dropped his weapon and raised his hands in the air. As soon as the "mop" hit the floor, Dr. Ickle began giving orders.

"Grab him, you idiots," Ickle shouted at the goons. "Chain him like the beast he is, and lock him up in the holding cell. Grab the other two as well."

"You heard the Doc." Fat Neck shoved Skinny and the other goons in front. "Now do what he ordered."

"Yeah." Skinny shoved the other goons too. "You heard the Doc. Get him!"

Slowly, the three goons turned toward Nicky. They approached him cautiously, as if Nicky were a bomb about to explode.

This is nuts, Nicky thought. These guys seemed more afraid of him than he was of them. And they were the ones with the guns.

Nicky scanned the room, trying to figure out what to do. That was when he noticed Zoe's face.

Her mouth was turned upside down, and her forehead was crinkling into one giant wrinkle.

Nicky started to sweat. It was definitely not the look he wanted to see. In fact, it was the look that was bound to get them killed.

Don't do it, Zoe! Nicky's brain screamed.

He tried to make eye contact with Zoe. He tried to get it through her head that this was not the time or the place for one of her monster tantrums.

But Zoe wasn't getting the message. She was way too busy squeezing her eyes shut and puffing out her cheeks.

No doubt about it. Zoe was going to blow!

Just then Ickle noticed that Zoe had started to turn blue. "What's this little alien doing?"

Zoe let it rip. *"Wwwwwwwaaaaaaaaahhhhhhhhh!"*

The sound started medium loud, like her usual

screams. But the wind from her lips quickly grew to gale force.

As the storm gathered strength, Nicky could feel his face begin to vibrate. He stuck his fingers in his ears. But still, his eardrums began to implode.

"WWWWWWAAAAAAAAHHHHHHHH!"

The second, skull-smashing blow hit the airwaves. Zoe was just warming up.

For a second, Nicky wished that Fat Neck and his goons really would start firing, just to put him out of his misery.

But Fat Neck and his goons didn't shoot. Instead, they freaked.

"AAAAAGGGGHHHHHH!" Fat Neck cried, covering his blubbery ear holes. "Somebody help me! My head's about to explode!"

"Help *you*?" Skinny shot back. "My eyeballs are popping out!"

"Let me out of here!" the other aliens shouted, dropping their weapons and running for the door.

"Me first!" Ickle insisted, shoving past them.

Nicky couldn't believe It. The aliens were actually tripping over themselves to get away from Zoe! He watched in amazement as they tumbled through the door, then ran for their lives.

The only alien who didn't run was Rachael. She was cowering in the corner, looking terrified.

"Oh, man!" Rachael murmured, glancing nervously at Zoe. "What other killer alien powers does she have?"

Nicky almost laughed. While Zoe was definitely enough to scare the wits out of anyone, she was hardly a killer.

"You don't have to be afraid of her," Nicky assured Rachael. "She's not trying to kill anybody. She's just, uh . . . a little noisy."

But Rachael still looked terrified—until Zoe started screaming in the aliens' language.

"I want my mommy and daddy!" she wailed.

Instantly, Rachael's big blue eyes filled with that strange gooey liquid again.

"Oh, you poor little thing." Rachael hurried over and wrapped her long, skinny arms around Zoe. "Of course you want your mommy and daddy. And I'm going to bring you to them." She lifted Zoe from the slab.

"Really?" Zoe squealed.

"Really," Rachael answered, giving Zoe a hug.

"My name is Zoe," Zoe told her. "What's yours?"

"Rachael," she answered, showing the white rocks in her mouth.

"That's my brother, Nicolai," Zoe pointed out. "But we call him Nicky."

"I know that's your brother," Rachael said. "I just didn't know what his name was."

Nicky felt embarrassed. For once, Zoe had better manners than he did. "Sorry." Nicky shrugged. "With everything that was going on, I guess I forgot to tell you my name."

"Don't worry about it," Rachael said. "We were kind of busy."

Nicky smiled. He was beginning to think Rachael really was a cool alien.

"Where are my mom and dad?" Zoe wanted to know.

"In Lab Number Six," Rachael answered. "Come on," she told Nicky, carrying Zoe through the door. "We'll take the elevator up, just in case the stairs are crawling with creeps."

Nicky followed Rachael and Zoe through the dark basement to two steel doors. Next to the doors was a neon light with two big red buttons. When Rachael pushed the circular button on top, the doors quickly slid open.

"Get in," she said, stepping inside what looked like a giant glass tube. "This will take us up to Level Six."

Nicky peered nervously at the strange glass tube, wishing they could take the stairs. At least he had the hang of those.

But Nicky wasn't about to argue with the one alien he was actually beginning to trust. He climbed into the tube, and the steel doors sealed shut again. Within moments, the surface beneath their feet shot them upward.

As the tube rose out of the basement, Nicky couldn't believe his eyes.

The alien elevator wasn't traveling *inside* the building like a regular elevator. It was traveling on the *outside*! Nicky was suddenly looking out over a strange new world.

CHAPTER 9

"Whoa!" Nicky exclaimed, pointing to a fiery globe suspended in midair. The beams shooting off the orb were filtering through the glass and warming up the tube. "What is that?" he asked Rachael.

"The sun," Rachael answered.

"The sun?" Zoe laughed. "That's not the sun! That's like a flying fireball."

"Nope. It's our sun," Rachael informed them.

"And what's that?" Zoe asked, pointing below.

"That's Earth," Rachael announced.

"Earth?" Nicky echoed. "No way."

He pressed his face against the glass, trying to see the landscape below. Rachael had called it "Earth," but it looked more like a tar pit, he thought, with mutant-looking trees shooting out of the gooey black ground.

Nicky could also see dozens of alien vehicles zooming across the strange surface, and then docking between rectangular lines that had been painted on the surface.

Nicky watched as one alien after the other climbed out of the transports and headed toward the building.

"Look!" Nicky cried out in horror as he spotted a group of aliens heading *away* from the building. "There's my mom and dad, with Fat Neck and Skinny! And Ickle the Iceman is with them too!"

Rachael quickly craned her neck around Nicky to see. "Oh my gosh!" she gasped. "They're taking them away!"

"To where?" Nicky asked.

"I don't know," Rachael answered. "But it doesn't look good."

Mr. and Mrs. Gogol were being led to a boxlike transport with metal bars. They were chained together like animals, and they moved along in a daze, as if drugged.

Fat Neck kept shoving Nicky's mom in the back with his gun to get her to move faster. She almost fell down.

"Hey!" Nicky shouted, pounding on the glass tube. "Leave her alone!" But Fat Neck kept shoving.

"Do something!" Nicky told Rachael.

"Like what?" Rachael asked.

"I don't know," Nicky cried. "Can't you beam through this glass and stop them?"

"No!" Rachael shot back. "What do you think I am, a magician?"

Fat Neck and Skinny loaded Nicky's parents into the barred transport. Dr. Ickle climbed in too. In a millisecond, the transport had taken off and was out of sight.

"I want my mommy and daddy!" Zoe started to wail again.

"Wait a minute. I've got an idea!" Rachael frantically pushed a green button on the neon panel inside the elevator. "Come on, you stupid thing!" she shouted. "Go back to Level One!"

Suddenly, the elevator began to descend, dropping so fast, Nicky's head hit the glass ceiling. A moment later, the tube jerked to a stop.

"Level One," a computerized voice announced. "Exit through the glass doors to your right for company parking, exit left for the lobby."

"We're going to the right," Rachael instructed them. "We have to follow the transport. It's the only hope we have of saving your parents!" Still holding Zoe, she stepped out of the tube onto the creepy black goo.

For a moment, Nicky was afraid to move. Zoe was safe because she was being carried. But it looked as if Nicky's feet would get swallowed up as soon as they touched the ground.

"Are you coming or not?" Rachael demanded.

Nicky didn't want to get sucked up by an alien tar pit. But his parents were in terrible danger; he couldn't afford to waste another second. He took a deep breath, then followed Rachael out onto the black terrain.

To Nicky's amazement, the ground beneath his feet wasn't as gooey as it looked. In fact, it seemed pretty solid. Nicky even jumped up and down, testing it.

"Will you hurry up already?" Rachael huffed. "Before they sic the militia on us."

"The militia?" Zoe repeated. "What's that?"

"Trust me," Rachael said. "You don't want to know."

"Are they the police?" Nicky asked.

"Worse," Rachael told him. "And they've probably been given orders to shoot you on sight! Now run!"

With that news, Nicky took off behind Rachael and Zoe with the speed of a rocket. He kept up with Rachael as she zigzagged around dozens of strange-looking transports.

"We'll take Uncle Ickle's four-wheeler," Rachael screamed over her shoulder. "I've got the keys!"

"Is it fast?" Nicky asked.

"Yeah," Rachael called back. "It flies like the wind."

Rachael stopped in front of what looked like a Land Rover. But it was big and black and shaped more like a tank.

"Uh-oh," Rachael cried suddenly. "We've got one small problem."

"What's that?" Nicky asked.

"I don't know how to drive," Rachael answered.

"What do you mean, you don't know how to drive?" Nicky yelped.

"I don't have my license yet," Rachael told him. "I'm only twelve, you know!"

"Well, that's just terrific," Nicky moaned. "Now what are we going to do?"

"Why can't *you* drive it?" Zoe asked Nicky. "You already know how to fly."

Rachael's eyes lit up. "You know how to fly?"

"I don't know how to fly alien transports!" Nicky shot back.

"It's not that hard to drive this thing—I can probably talk you through it," Rachael went on. "I've watched Uncle Ickle drive a thousand times."

"Then why don't you drive it yourself?" Nicky asked.

"Because I'll get arrested!" Rachael suddenly rolled her blue eyes. "It's against the law to drive when you're twelve."

"Yeah?" Nicky shot back. "Well, I'm twelve too!"

"But you're an alien," Rachael pointed out. "They're not going to arrest you."

"Oh, right," Nicky snapped. "They're only going to shoot me!"

Just then, a souped-up, cherry-red alien machine flew into the space next to the four-wheeler. It came to a stop so quickly, Nicky could actually see its rubbery landing gear smoking.

"Uh-oh!" Rachael's eyes went wide. "I think we've got problems."

Nicky's heart pounded wildly as the smoky gray glass on the side of the ship slid open. *This is it,* he told himself. *It's over.* A wrinkled, squished face popped out of the hole. "Excuse me," the creature croaked like a frog. "Can you tell me how to get to the Planet X Cafe? It's Oldie's Night, and I don't want to miss it."

Nicky almost burst out laughing. This guy didn't want to shoot them—he needed directions!

The creature was studying a sheet of paper. "According to this map, I should be there already. But my eyes aren't so good. And I can't seem to find my magnifying lenses."

Rachael put Zoe down. She moved closer to the alien, carefully shielding both Zoe and Nicky.

"The Planet X Cafe is just past the Galaxy Diner," she told the wrinkled, squished head. "Keep going north until you come to the clover." She pointed out over the tar pit. "You'll see it straight down on your left."

Planet X? Nicky thought suddenly. *Is that where we are?*

If so, Nicky reasoned, he was way out of his own solar system. He'd never even heard of Planet X.

Nicky racked his brains for a second, trying to remember what he'd learned in Astronomy. But he was certain that Planet X was so far from home, it hadn't even been charted yet.

The wrinkled alien thanked Rachael, then rummaged around for something. "Oh, here they are," he murmured.

Before Nicky realized what was happening, the alien had found his lenses and put them on. His bug eyes bugged out of his head.

"Jumping Jehoshaphat!" the creature croaked as he spotted Nicky and Zoe. "We're being invaded by aliens! Run, little girl," he shouted at Rachael. "Run for your life!"

"They're not going to hurt you." Rachael tried to calm him down.

But the creature was already reaching for the radio device that hung from the control panel in front of him.

Nicky felt his pulse beating wildly.

Frog Head was alerting the whole alien nation. In another few minutes the militia would swoop in for the kill!

CHAPTER 10

"We've got to get out of here!" Rachael shouted, tossing something to Nicky.

"What's this?" Nicky asked.

"Keys!" Rachael cried, scooping up Zoe again. "Now are you going to drive this thing or not?"

There wasn't much of a choice, not when Frog Head was still croaking away into his transmitter.

"Okay, okay," Nicky told her. "I'll do it!"

"Then hurry up and get in!" Rachael ordered.

Nicky quickly scanned the side of Ickle's transport, looking for some kind of latch release. "Hey, Rachael," he finally said in a panic. "How the heck do you get these hatches open?"

"With the button on the keys!" Rachael was panicking too. "The locks should automatically open."

Great, Nicky thought. *I'm not even inside the cockpit yet, and we're already off to a disastrous start.*

Nicky pushed the button attached to the key ring, and there was a loud *click* as the hatches immediately unlocked.

Rachael didn't wait for Nicky to figure out how to actually open them. Instead, she slid the hatches away herself, pulling three silver levers built into their sides.

"I'm going to put Zoe in the back," she told Nicky. "It's safer back there."

Nicky watched as Rachael plunked Zoe down on what looked like a cushioned black bench and secured her with lots of straps and buckles. Then he climbed into the front of the transport and strapped himself in tightly too.

Rachael quickly sealed off the hatch, then joined him in the cockpit.

"Okay," she said, pointing to a silver hole on the control panel. "Just slide the black key into that hole and turn it to your right. The engine should kick right in."

With a nervous glance at Frog Head, Nicky did as he was told.

The engine kicked in all right—but Nicky's heart stopped.

Thunder rolling through the heavens was nowhere near as terrifying as the sound of the alien four-wheeler roaring to life.

"Oh, man!" Nicky cried. "This thing sounds like it's going to explode."

That was definitely the wrong thing to say with Zoe within earshot.

"I DON'T WANT TO EXPLODE!" she wailed from the backseat.

"It's okay, Zoe." Rachael craned her neck around to reassure Zoe. "No one's going to explode." Then she shot Nicky a dirty look.

Nicky got the "how-could-you-be-so-stupid" message loud and clear. So he decided to keep quiet when a bunch of glowing lights flashed on the control panel.

"Okay." Rachael was obviously trying to sound calm. "Now just pull back this lever and push those three pedals."

Nicky swallowed hard as he studied his instruments.

The "lever" seemed easy enough to work, because the flying positions were clearly marked. But the pedals were a whole other story.

"What do the pedals do?" Nicky finally had no choice but to ask.

"One of them increases your speed," Rachael explained. "One slows you down or makes you stop. And the other has something to do with the gears."

"Which one is which?" Nicky asked.

Rachael hesitated. "I'm not sure," she admitted. "I guess you're just going to have to figure that out as we go."

"What?" Nicky shrieked. These were hardly the blow-by-blow instructions Nicky was hoping for. But there was no time for him to search for a manual. Thanks to Frog Head, there were already strange-looking ships circling around.

Nicky's heart pounded as he pulled back the lever and pushed down a pedal. "Hang on, Zoe! We're about to take off!"

The four-wheeler shot forward. But it didn't go upward, as Nicky had expected. Instead it raced directly across the tar pit.

"You did it!" Rachael shrieked, bouncing up and down in her seat. "You're driving!"

"I thought you said this thing *flew*," Nicky snapped.

"It does," Rachael told him. "It flies along the ground!"

Nicky had to admit that it *felt* as if they were flying. The four-wheeler zoomed across the dark terrain so fast, there seemed to be no contact at all with the ground.

That was a problem. Especially when the tar pit below suddenly opened into what looked like an alien freeway— cram-packed with ground-flying transports.

"Nicky! Watch out!" Rachael cried, as they sped out into oncoming traffic.

Unfortunately, Rachael's screams came too late.

This time, Nicky Gogol really *was* going to crash.

CHAPTER 11

"Turn the wheel!" Rachael screamed over Zoe's deafening wails.

"What wheel?" Nicky cried in a panic.

"The wheel in front of you!" Rachael cried back.

"Turn it how?"

"Any way you want!" Rachael said hysterically. "Just turn it before we get creamed!"

Nicky grabbed the wheel on the control panel and turned it fast and hard to the left.

"*AAAAAAAAAGGGGGGGGGGHHHHHHHHH!*" Zoe's screams reached tantrum proportions as the four-wheeler spun out of control. "WE'RE GOING TO DIE! WE'RE GOING TO . . ."

It was then that Nicky realized he should have spun the wheel to the right. Zoe's screams were suddenly drowned out by the sound of the four-wheeler scraping against another big metal object.

"Duck!" Rachael shouted as their transport shot under the enormous chunk of steel passing overhead.

Nicky was sure that the top of the transport would be sheared right off, along with their heads!

But neither one of those things happened.

Instead, the four-wheeler slid under the sixteen-wheeled flying machine and came out the other side, with barely a dent.

Nicky slammed his foot down on pedal number three, the one he hoped would stop them completely.

Thankfully, it did.

As the transport came to a stop, there was complete silence. That really scared Nicky.

"Zoe!" He spun around in his seat. "Are you okay?"

Zoe just nodded, looking totally spooked.

"What about you?" Nicky asked Rachael.

"I'm fine," Rachael said. "Just a little shaken up."

"Thank goodness no one was hurt," Nicky sighed.

Even the driver behind the wheel of the huge chunk of steel seemed to be fine. In fact, he turned his transport around and pulled up next to Nicky.

"Is everyone okay down there?" he shouted through an opening in his hatch six feet above them.

This alien's awfully friendly, Nicky thought.

"Hey, Rachael," he started. "How do I open the porthole in here so I can tell him we're okay?"

"Are you nuts?" Rachael shrieked. "If that guy finds out

that he just had an accident with an alien, he'll freak! Don't open a thing!"

Nicky hesitated. Rachael had a point, but he didn't want to be unfriendly.

"Go, Nicky!" Zoe chimed in. "Go, GO, GOOOOOOOOOOO!"

Nicky came to his senses and shoved the lever into reverse. Then he burned rubber, leaving the big rig back in the dust.

"We've got to get off this freeway," Rachael said. "There's too much traffic. We might get spotted."

"I know," Nicky agreed, swerving out of the way of yet another alien transport. "And driving this thing isn't as easy as you said it would be."

"It's not your driving I'm worried about—" Rachael said. But she didn't finish her thought because she suddenly spotted an exit. "Turn here!" she ordered, pointing to the right.

Nicky did his best to make a clean break from the traffic. Still, he tilted dangerously left before he finally swerved to the right.

Within seconds, they were traveling through a deserted stretch of alien terrain.

"Is this the path that's going to take us to my mom and dad?" Zoe wanted to know.

Rachael was quiet.

"Well, is it?" Nicky asked.

Rachael shrugged.

"I thought you said we were going to follow my parents." Nicky was beginning to get nervous.

"I said we would *try* to follow your parents," Rachael corrected him. "But I never said we would actually find them."

Nicky's blood began to chill, along with the tone of Rachael's voice.

"So where are we going?" Zoe started to cry.

"To my grandmother's house," Rachael answered. "Where I should have been all along."

CHAPTER 12

Nicky's heart clenched in his chest as tightly as his fingers were clenched around the wheel.

Rachael wasn't trying to help him find his parents! She was trying to get to her grandmother's house! And she was using Nicky to do it!

How could I have been so stupid? he thought. *No one in their right mind would ever trust an alien. No one but me!*

Nicky glanced nervously at Rachael, who was suddenly looking more like a smug, creepy creature than a warm-hearted friend.

Oh, man! Nicky's brain warped into light speed. *What if I was right all along? What if Rachael really does work for Ickle? And what if Ickle works for Grandma?*

Fear tore through Nicky's chest the way Ickle wanted to tear through his skull.

What if Grandma's like the biggest head on Planet X?

Nicky continued to freak. *Or worse still, what if Grandma doesn't even have a head? What if she's just a giant walking brain who's masterminded everything?*

Nicky jerked the wheel of the transport—hard.

"What are you doing?" Rachael screeched, along with the transport as it spun one hundred eighty degrees.

"I'm going back to the freeway!" Nicky told her. "No way I'm facing a giant alien brain!"

"What are you talking about?" Rachael cried.

"Your grandmother," Nicky replied. "She's the master-mind, isn't she? And you're just following Ickle's orders. You've been trying to trick us into thinking you're some kind of alien friend. But you're really a cold-hearted icegirl, just like your uncle!"

Rachael looked like she'd been shot with a stun gun. Then Zoe's panic alarm went off.

"AAAAAGGGGGGGHHHHHHHH!" she wailed. "I DON'T WANT TO GO TO A GIANT BRAIN'S HOUSE!"

"My grandmother's not a giant brain!" Rachael insisted, trying to calm Zoe down. "In fact, everyone thinks she belongs with the noo-noos!"

"Oh, yeah?" Nicky shot back. "Then how come you're taking us there, huh? How come we're not flying around this planet looking for my parents like you said we would?"

"We're not flying around this planet looking for your parents because it's starting to get dark," Rachael shouted. She pointed to the fiery globe that was quickly dropping from the sky. "Besides, I don't know where they are. I'm taking you to my grandmother's house because she's the only one on this planet who will help us!"

Nicky didn't know what to believe anymore. And he certainly didn't know what to do.

"Now," Rachael huffed, "are you going to turn this thing around, or are you trying to get us all killed?"

"I DON'T WANT TO GET KILLED!" Zoe started wailing a brand-new tune, right in Nicky's ear. "TURN AROUND, NICKY! TURN US AROUND!"

"Okay, okay!" Nicky cried, quickly spinning the wheel. "We'll get ourselves killed at Grandma's house if that's what it takes to shut you up! Now SHUT UP!" He practically bit Zoe's head off.

The moment the transport spun back around, Zoe's lungs took a break. But Nicky's heart went into overdrive as soon as he saw the terrifying terrain.

"So this is the way to your grandmother's house, huh?" he managed to choke out.

"Yup," Rachael answered. "It's right past this desert—over the horizon out there."

The "desert" was unlike any stretch of land Nicky had ever seen. Miles of tiny crystal-like stones covered the ground like a rock carpet. Strange-looking life formations reached for the sky with long prickly arms.

The "horizon" was even more terrifying than the terrain. Particularly because the fiery globe was plummeting straight for the meteor mountain standing in front of it.

"Isn't there any other way to go?" Nicky asked. "This

way looks pretty bumpy. Not to mention kind of hot," he added, watching the fireball falling ahead.

"No," Rachael told him. "This is the easiest route."

But Rachael was mistaken. This wasn't an easy route at all. And Nicky was about to find out that the road to Grandma's house was definitely going to be more than bumpy.

CHAPTER 13

Please let us get through this, Nicky prayed, pushing the speed pedal as hard as he could. If they had to cross an alien desert, climb over a meteor mountain, then pass through a fireball to get to "grandmother's house," Nicky definitely wanted to fly as fast as he could.

Sure enough, they weren't traveling for more than a minute when a natural disaster struck. But it didn't come from outside their transport.

"Nicky," Zoe whined. "I have to go to the bathroom."

"Not for real," Nicky groaned under his breath.

"Yes, for real!" Zoe heard him anyway.

Nicky shot Rachael a look. "Please tell me there's some kind of bathroom facility in this transport," he said.

Rachael shook her head.

"Nothing?" Nicky pressed. "Not even a portable one?"

Rachael shook her head again. "Nobody goes to the bathroom while they're traveling," she informed him. "You're supposed to go *before* you take off."

"Terrific," Nicky grumbled. "This is just what I need."

"Niiiiii-cky!" Zoe's cry became more insistent. "I HAVE TO GO!"

"Can't you just hold it a little bit longer?" Nicky asked hopelessly.

"No-oooooo!" Zoe shot back. "I have to go now!"

"Well, you can't go now!" Nicky informed her. "I mean, what do you want me to do, pull over in the middle of this desert?"

"Yes!" Zoe cried, squiggling in her seat. "I'm as full as an ocean! I'm about to go in my pants!"

That was all Rachael needed to hear to join in the panic. "Pull over!" she shouted at Nicky. "She's as full as an ocean, and this is a tiny vehicle!"

"Okay, okay," Nicky shouted back. "Everybody just calm down!"

He quickly maneuvered their transport to a smooth strip of desert. Then he coasted to a stop.

"There," he told Zoe. "Now get out and go."

"I'm not going out there by myself!" Zoe cried. "It's pitch-black outside!"

It was true. The fireball had completely disappeared behind the meteor mountain, leaving a strange, eerie blackness covering the desert like a heavy blanket. Even the lights on the transport couldn't seem to penetrate the darkness.

"Rachael will go with you, won't you, Rachael?" Nicky pleaded.

The look on Rachael's face told Nicky that she wasn't too happy about getting out of the transport either. And this was her planet!

"Why don't *you* take her," Rachael insisted. "She's *your* sister, after all."

"Yeah, but you're a girl," Nicky argued. "You should take her."

"I don't care who takes me," Zoe screamed. "But somebody better take me—NOW!"

Rachael quickly released the hatch on her side of the transport. "Okay, okay," she said, stepping out into the dusty, dry darkness. "I'll take you."

Nicky heaved a sigh of relief as Rachael opened Zoe's hatch and unhooked Zoe from her seat. The moment Zoe was on her feet, Rachael said, "Go, and hurry!"

"I can't go here," Zoe complained. "Everyone will see me!"

"No one will see you," Nicky snapped. "There's nobody out there!" At least he hoped no one was out there.

"I want to go behind a bush or something," Zoe informed them.

"There are no bushes out here," Rachael told her, "just those trees over there." She pointed to the strange life formations with long prickly arms.

"Then I'll go behind them," Zoe insisted.

Nicky buried his face in his hands. He couldn't believe this was happening.

"Fine." Rachael was losing her patience too. "Let's just do it fast, okay? Wait here," she told Nicky. "And don't cut off that engine. The last thing we want to do is get ourselves stuck out here."

"No argument from me," Nicky agreed.

But leaving the engine running was a big, big mistake. Zoe was full—but their fuel tank was not.

CHAPTER 14

"Warning!" A computerized voice cut through the silence inside the transport as red lights flashed on the control panel. "Your fuel level is low."

If Nicky hadn't been strapped to his seat, he would have gone right through the ceiling.

"You've got to be kidding me!" he cried, staring at the flashing red lights. The needle on the fuel gauge was quickly dropping to *E*.

"Repeat," the voice warned again. "Your fuel level is low. You are approaching Empty."

"Now what?" Nicky yelped. He thought about turning the engine off. But he was afraid that if he did that, the engine would never start up again.

I'm going to kill Zoe for this, Nicky thought, groping to find the switch that would open the smoky gray glass to his right. Maybe he could yell to Zoe and Rachael and get them back here.

But as he flipped the switches, his panic grew.

One of the switches turned off the lights inside the transport, while another one killed the lights on the outside.

Just open the hatch, Nicky finally told himself, reaching for the silver lever on his side of the transport.

The hatch immediately slid open, and he jumped out. Outside, it was pitch-black and there was no sign of Zoe and Rachael.

Oh, man. Nicky freaked as he stepped onto the crystallized grains that covered the ground. *We're going to die out here. I just know it.*

Suddenly, his foot sank below the rocky surface. The "desert" was far worse than the tar pit! This ground really was going to swallow him whole!

Nicky yanked his foot from the ground and shot forward with the speed of sound. "Guys!" he cried, running across the sucking soil toward the mutant trees. "We've got to get out of here! We're running out of fuel!"

The only reply from the trees was a strange rattling sound.

What the heck is that? Nicky stopped dead in his tracks.

The answer slithered out of the blackness and tore across the crystals.

"Aaaaaaaggghhhh!" Nicky wailed. "There's a giant alien worm out here! Somebody help me!"

The giant alien worm took one look at Nicky and headed off in the opposite direction.

A moment later, something even bigger crept out of the trees.

"What are you screaming about?" Rachael sounded pretty jittery herself.

"Worms." Nicky could barely squeak out the word. "And fuel!"

"What about fuel?"

"We're running out of it!" Nicky informed her.

With that news, Rachael reached behind the trees with her long skinny arm and pulled Zoe out by her neck.

"Hey!" Zoe protested. She was wiggling like the alien worm as she struggled to adjust her clothes. "What are you doing?"

"Getting us out of here," Rachael told her, taking off for the transport with Zoe in tow.

Nicky was two steps behind.

"I think there's a filling station over the mountain," Rachael told Nicky as she threw Zoe into the back. "If we can just make it a little bit farther, we ought to be fine."

That was a very big "if." Especially since the engine's roar had died to a hum.

"Just floor it!" Rachael said as she and Nicky strapped themselves in.

To Nicky's surprise, the transport took off. Within minutes, they were heading over the mountain.

But suddenly the engine began to cough and spit. Nicky checked the fuel gauge. Sure enough, the needle had fallen below *E.*

"Hang on!" Nicky cried.

Seconds later, they started to drop down the side of the mountain.

CHAPTER
15

"What the heck is that?" Nicky yelped as they rolled down the side of the mountain toward a glowing glass structure that rose from its base.

"That's the filling station!" Rachael shrieked.

"The filling station?" Nicky echoed. "Really?"

"Yeah," Rachael said, pointing to a giant blob of light sitting on a huge metal pole. "Can't you read the sign?"

"No," Nicky shot back. Speaking the aliens' language was one thing, but reading it was a whole different story.

"It says, 'Seemor's Sunco,'" Rachael informed him.

Nicky's brain tried to process that information, but it didn't make sense. "What's Seemor?" he finally asked.

"I guess it's the name of the guy who owns the filling station," Rachael answered with a shrug.

"And Sunco is fuel?" Nicky asked.

"Yeah," Rachael said. "Sunco—the Sun Company. Don't you get it?"

"No," Nicky said. He wasn't sure he wanted to get it, either. The only sun Nicky had seen on this planet was a hot ball of flame. No way he wanted to fill up with that.

Nicky braked to a stop near several huge metal towers that rose out of the ground in front of the glowing glass square. Two laser beams crisscrossed the sky above them. Nicky was relieved they'd at least arrived safely—until Seemor stepped up to their transport.

"What'll it be?" the alien demanded.

This time, Nicky didn't want to find the switch that opened his hatch. Not only was Seemor as big and as ugly as Fat Neck, his alien nose holes were humongous, and dripping like crazy.

Nicky felt nauseated—especially when Seemor wiped the green, gloppy gunk from his nose with the back of his greasy fat hand.

"Hit that button," Rachael told Nicky, pointing to a tiny switch by his arm. "Then tell him we want to fill it up."

Nicky just stared at her. "Aren't you forgetting something?"

"Like what?" Rachael asked.

"Like he's going to freak out when he sees me sitting in the driver's seat!"

"You're right," Rachael agreed. "I forgot for a second." She quickly reached under her seat and pulled out a cloak. "Here. Put this on," she instructed. "And cover your face with the hood."

Before Nicky could protest, Rachael was pressing the button to open the hatch.

"Wait a minute!" Nicky cried, struggling to put on the cloak.

Luckily, he managed to cover his face before Seemor saw more than he should have.

"So what'll it be, friend?" Seemor's breath smelled like foot fungus as it floated into Nicky's nostrils.

"Fill it up." Nicky repeated what Rachael had said.

"You want premium Sunco, or regular?" Seemor wanted to know.

"Which one has the least amount of flames?" Nicky asked nervously.

Rachael jabbed him in the ribs. "Just take the regular," she whispered under her breath.

"The regular," Nicky informed Seemor.

"You've got it," Seemor said, turning to reach for a huge black tube.

Just then, Zoe popped her head over the top of Nicky's seat. "I'm hungry," she grumbled, as loudly as her stomach.

Seemor looked back at the transport.

"Get down, Zoe!" Rachael hissed.

"But I'm hungry!" Zoe shouted.

Rachael quickly covered Zoe's mouth as Seemor took a step toward the hatch. Then she shoved Zoe hard as Seemor stuck his fat face through the hatch hole.

"Did I hear somebody in this vehicle say they were hungry?" he asked.

"I did," Rachael blurted, struggling to keep Zoe quiet and hidden. "Actually, my husband and I are both hungry."

My husband? Nicky cringed. *Are you nuts?* He shot Rachael a look.

So did Seemor. Then he eyed them both curiously.

"Anyway," Rachael rambled nervously, "would you know where we could get something to eat around here?"

"Right through those doors," Seemor said, pointing to the glowing square behind the towers. "Why don't you take the little lady inside," he suggested to Nicky, "while I finish fueling your tank."

Now what? Nicky gulped.

"Why don't you wait here, honey," Rachael said, patting Nicky's arm. "There's no reason we both have to go."

Honey? Nicky gagged, but he played along. "Good idea, uh, sweetheart." He choked on the word.

"Not if you ask me," Seemor butted in. "In fact, I think it's mighty rude to send the little lady in there all by herself," he told Nicky.

This from an alien who didn't use tissues!

"What are we going to do?" Nicky murmured as Seemor turned back to the tube.

"I guess we should both go in there together," Rachael said.

"What about Zoe?" Nicky asked.

"She'll have to stay here," Rachael answered. She turned around and gave Zoe strict instructions to stay hidden.

Nicky cautiously stepped out of the transport. Luckily, the cloak Rachael had found was so long, it dragged along the ground while he walked, hiding his feet.

Still, Seemor kept watching curiously as Nicky followed Rachael toward the doors of the glowing glass square.

"I'm not so sure this is such a good idea," Nicky whispered. "Seemor is looking at me like he knows something's fishy."

"Don't worry about it," Rachael said calmly. "We're just going to grab some munchies and get out of here," she told him, reaching for the door. "Keep your head down and your hood up, and no one will notice you."

"If you say so," Nicky sighed, following Rachael into the alien food store.

But they'd barely taken one step before Rachael stopped dead in her tracks.

"Oh, no!" she gasped, pointing to a strange white box with pictures flashing across its lighted surface.

Nicky nearly jumped out of his cloak as he recognized the images moving across the screen.

Rachael was wrong. Everyone on Planet X was going to notice Nicky. Even with his head down and his hood up, there was no way for Nicky to hide his face—not when it was plastered all over the alien news!

CHAPTER 16

Nicky listened in horror as an alien voice filtered through the box.

"While the government denies reports of an alien crash, this footage, taken by our own WPX news team, clearly shows that there is some kind of official cover-up going on," the voice reported.

"That's me!" Nicky cried as he watched another image of himself flash up on the box. He was being carried out of the same gray craft that had sucked their plane into its belly. But he wasn't awake. He was lying unconscious on what looked like an alien rubber band stretched across two giant brown match sticks.

Fat Neck and Skinny were carrying the poles.

"I can't believe this," Rachael shrieked. "Thanks to WPX, the whole planet is going to know you're here!"

"But that guy is lying!" Nicky suddenly felt angry. "We didn't crash! That gray thing swallowed us whole. We were abducted!"

Just then, a horrible voice startled them both.

"Hey!"

Nicky spun to see a blubbery alien rolling straight for them.

"What do you two think you're doing over there?" the alien shouted.

"We're not doing anything," Rachael declared. "We were just watching the news."

"Oh, yeah?" the alien growled. "Well, this isn't a news station. This here's a store. And if you two aren't buying anything, I'll call my husband, Seemor, in here to get rid of you both."

"No," Rachael yelped. "You don't have to do that. We're buying stuff," she assured the blob.

Rachael grabbed Nicky's arm and pulled him toward the back of the store.

"What the heck does she need Seemor for?" Nicky gulped. "All she has to do is sit on us and she'll smush us to death!"

"No kidding," Rachael agreed. "Now listen to me," she instructed in a panic. "Just start pulling some munchies off these shelves before she gets a better look at you and figures out that you're the alien on the news."

Nicky's stomach flipped at the thought. Then it flip-flopped again, the moment he caught sight of the "munchies."

"Oh, puke," Nicky cried, staring at a package of what looked like alien guts on a stick. "You don't really eat this stuff, do you?"

"That's beef jerky," Rachael informed him. "And it tastes really good."

"That's not beef!" Nicky winced. "And don't call me jerky!"

Rachael rolled her eyes at him as she reached for the package.

"And what the heck is this?" Nicky picked up a box of chunky brown blobs. "Alien poop?"

"They're Noogets," Rachael answered. "It's candy."

This time, Nicky rolled *his* eyes. Since when was alien poop candy?

"And what about this?" Nicky asked, picking up what he was sure was a bottle of blood.

"Could we stop with all the questions already?" Rachael said in a snippy tone. "Just grab what you can and let's beat it out of here."

"Fine," Nicky told her. He reached for the least disgusting-looking thing on the shelf—a bag of chewy, fat worms.

"Now," Rachael directed as they headed for the front of the store, "just do what I do. And keep your mouth shut."

Nicky followed her orders.

"We'll take all of this," Rachael told the blob. She plunked down her munchies.

Nicky put down his munchies too.

The blob stared at him curiously, scratching her

bloated, fat skull. "Don't I know you from somewhere?" she suddenly asked.

Rachael quickly stepped in front of Nicky. "I don't think so," she said. "My husband and I aren't from around these parts."

"That's funny," the blob said suspiciously. "Your husband looks awfully familiar."

Just then, a siren went off.

Nicky was sure it was some kind of "alien-in-the-food-store alarm"—until the blob started moaning about "coppers."

"What's that?" Nicky asked nervously.

"Coppers, you idiot," the blob repeated. "They're out there harassing my Seemor again." She pointed past the glowing glass. "One armed robbery and a skyjacking, and those coppers still treat him like a criminal," she huffed.

Nicky sighed with relief. It wasn't the "alien-in-the-food-store alarm." It was the "coppers-on-the-outside alarm"!

But that wasn't a good thing at all.

Because the "coppers" definitely weren't there to harass Seemor again.

CHAPTER
17

Out by Seemor, Nicky could see two giant aliens, dressed in blue. Their blue-and-white transport was docked directly behind Ickle's four-wheeler. On the top of the transport was a swirling red bubble, which seemed to be sounding the "copper alarm."

But the coppers themselves were what was most frightening. Around their waists they wore giant black straps, supporting an arsenal of weapons.

They had stun guns and chains, and dozens of small silver rockets ready to be launched from tiny black slots. And there were strange-looking bats—that had nothing to do with baseball.

Just the sight of the weapons was enough to make Nicky start shaking.

"This isn't good," Rachael mumbled nervously.

"You bet your little bippy this isn't good," the blob

moaned. "As a matter of fact, I'm going to put a stop to this nonsense once and for all. Those coppers aren't setting foot on my property anymore—not without an official search warrant."

Nicky wasn't quite sure what the blob was rambling on about. But getting rid of the "coppers" sounded like a pretty good idea.

Rachael thought so too. "You know what?" she said enthusiastically. "You *should* go out there and get rid of those coppers. No way they should be pushing poor Seemor around."

"You got that right!" The blob was clearly getting hot under her blubbery collar. "I'm definitely going to give them a piece of my mind, as soon as you pay for your goods."

Nicky looked at Rachael as the blob started running their munchies over a lighted "X" on the top of the counter and jamming everything into a white sack.

"You don't have to ring us up now," Rachael told the blob, swallowing hard. "We don't mind waiting until you get rid of the coppers."

"Just how stupid do you think I am?" the blob shot back. "If I go outside and leave the two of you in here alone, you'll probably steal me blind."

"We can't steal you blind if you take your eyeballs with you!" Nicky said. He'd just been trying to help. But Rachael looked as if she wanted to cut off his tongue.

The blubbery blob snorted loudly. "Now that's a good one," she said. "But I'm still not leaving you in here by yourselves. So you might as well just pay up." She stuck out her hand. "It comes to twenty-two smack-a-roos," she informed them.

Rachael's square chin hit her chest.

"I'm waiting," the blob sighed, sticking her hand out even farther.

Nicky had no idea what a "smack-a-roo" was, but he had the funny feeling they didn't have any.

"Pay up." The blob was losing patience. "Or I'll turn you over to those coppers out there."

"Oh, dear." Rachael's voice trembled. "I must have left my bag at home," she lied. "Check your pockets, honey," she told Nicky nervously. "Maybe we'll find what we need in there."

Nicky stuck his hands through the slits in the side of the cloak.

Please let there be smack-a-roos in this thing, he thought as he dug through the pouches that dropped straight to his knees.

A moment later, his fingers wrapped around what felt like a wad of sandy paper. He pulled it out of the cloak and showed it to Rachael. "Is this what we're looking for . . . honey?"

"Yes!" Rachael exclaimed. She grabbed the wad from Nicky's hand and peeled off three rectangular strips. "Here you go," she told the blob, handing her the smack-a-roos.

"And here you go," the blob said, cramming the sack of munchies in Rachael's face. Then she rolled around the counter and opened the glass door. "Now get out."

Nicky and Rachael stood frozen. No way either one of them wanted to go outside and face the coppers.

But the blob wouldn't budge without them. "Move it," she ordered. "I ain't got all night."

The two of them had no choice but to inch their way toward the door.

"The minute we get outside," Rachael whispered to Nicky, "get behind Seemor's wife. She's big enough to hide us both. If we're lucky, the cops won't see us, and *Mrs.* Seemor really will scare them away."

It wasn't much of a plan, but it was all they had.

"Hey, coppers!" the blob bellowed as she followed Nicky and Rachael outside. "What do you think you're doing over there with my Seemor?"

Nicky and Rachael scrambled to get behind her.

The moment they did, the coppers pulled their biggest weapons, their guns, from the straps around their waists.

"Get out of the way, Sally!" one of them shouted back. "This has nothing to do with you and Seemor."

Seemor and Sally? Not for real, Nicky thought.

"Don't even try to start playing those mind games with me," Sally the blob shouted back.

"We're not playing games," the other copper informed her. "You've got two fugitives hiding behind you. And if you don't roll out of our way, you're going to get hurt!"

"They're telling the truth, Sally," Seemor called out. "This here is a stolen vehicle." He pointed to Ickle's four-wheeler. "This time the coppers ain't accusing me."

With that news, Nicky and Rachael's protective shield bounced out of the way.

"Stay right where you are!" copper number one ordered as he stood poised to fire.

"And get those hands in the air!" copper number two added, striking the same pose.

Rachael dropped the sack of munchies to the ground and raised her arms above her head.

Nicky did the same. "What do we do now?" he hissed in a panic.

"I don't know," Rachael replied. "It's bad enough that they think we're thieves. But they're going to go ballistic when they find out you're an *alien* thief."

"I'm not an alien thief!" Nicky cried. "I'm not even an alien!"

Unfortunately, Nicky blurted that information a little too loudly.

"I knew you looked familiar!" Sally started to freak as she pointed her finger at Nicky. "That's not a vehicle snatcher! That's the alien from the news!" she announced.

"Dang!" Seemor started freaking out too. "I just pumped fuel for an alien! I ain't gonna get some kind of alien disease or something, am I, Sal?"

"You!" Copper number one pointed his weapon at Nicky. "Remove that hood! Now!"

Slowly, he began to obey. Out of the corner of his eye he saw the hatch to the four-wheeler slide open. Then Zoe slid out.

Nicky's heart tied itself into a knot that lodged in his throat. *Zoe, NO!* He wanted to scream as he tried to make eye contact. *Get back in the transport! Don't let them see you!*

If Nicky couldn't save his own life, he at least wanted to save Zoe's. But that wasn't going to happen.

"Look out!" Seemor shouted at the coppers. "There's a little alien behind you!"

The coppers spun around. "Hey!" they cried in unison. "It *is* a little alien!"

Luckily, it was a hungry little alien—who decided to unveil her most dangerous weapon.

"WHAAAAAAAAAAAAAAAAAAA!" Zoe wailed at the top of her lungs. "I'M STARVING TO DEATH! AND I'M TELLING MOMMY!"

At the sound of Zoe's voice, the coppers hit the dirt, covering their heads as if they were in the middle of a war zone.

Seemor and Sally did the same.

"Run!" Rachael ordered.

Nicky grabbed Zoe's arm and took off for the transport. But Seemor's hose was still sticking out of the side of it.

Now he had no choice but to run—and to keep running.

"Keep screaming, Zoe!" Nicky called out as he raced for the cover of darkness.

"I DON'T WANT TO KEEP SCREAMING!" Zoe wailed away. "I WANT TO GET SOMETHING TO EAT!"

"Well, you're not getting something to eat," Nicky snapped. "Not until we climb over that meteor mountain!"

"I DON'T WANT TO CLIMB OVER THE METEOR MOUNTAIN!" Zoe's voice started to rise.

And then so did the coppers.

Within seconds, they were back on their feet, and the blue-and-white transport was heading right for Nicky and Zoe.

CHAPTER 18

"Nooooooo!" Nicky cried as he scooped Zoe up and ran for the hills.

But there was no way Nicky was going to outrun the blue-and-white transport. In fact, the swirling red bubble was spinning so close to his back, Nicky could feel the heat from its light.

The coppers were going to run them down and then shoot! Or maybe they were just going to stab Nicky and Zoe with a couple of tranquilizer darts and bring them back to Ickle!

But to Nicky's surprise, the blue-and-white transport tore past them.

Nicky stopped in his tracks. "We're safe!" he said.

Then he noticed the blue-and-white spin to a stop, blocking their path.

The coppers weren't going to blast Nicky and Zoe away from behind! They were going to blow them away face-to-face!

Nicky clung to Zoe tightly. "Don't look, Zoe," he told her, burying her face in his shoulder. "It will all be over in a second."

Nicky closed his eyes so he wouldn't have to see their gruesome ending.

But this wasn't the end.

Nicky knew it the moment he heard Rachael's voice.

"Nicky!" she shrieked from the open hatch on the driver's side of the transport. "What are you doing? Get in already!"

Nicky couldn't believe his eyes. The coppers weren't chasing them—Rachael was!

"What are you doing with the coppers' transport?" Nicky shouted as he quickly opened the passenger's hatch and shoved Zoe in.

"I stole it," Rachael answered matter-of-factly. "Right out from under their noses," she added. "Actually, their noses were buried in dirt, thanks to Zoe."

"No way you stole the coppers' transport!" Nicky exclaimed as he climbed in himself.

"There wasn't a choice," Rachael said. "If I hadn't stolen this vehicle, you and Zoe would both be mud."

So that's what the alien guns do, Nicky thought. *They turn you into mud.*

Just then, Rachael hit the speed pedal hard.

"Geez, oh, man," Nicky cried, holding on for dear life.

"I thought you said you couldn't drive one of these!"

"I didn't think I could," Rachael told him. "But I'm doing pretty well, aren't I?"

Nicky didn't have the heart to say no. So he nodded and forced himself to smile weakly as Rachael zig-zagged her way through what looked like an alien jungle. The air was thick with mist, and strange-looking plants with feathery leaves were everywhere.

As the transport whizzed past, long, leafy vines seemed to reach up for it.

The jungle was so creepy, Nicky was suddenly glad that Rachael was driving as fast as she was.

"Where are we going?" Nicky asked, as their vehicle tore the arms off a vine.

"To my grandmother's house," Rachael reminded him.

"Are we almost there?" Zoe piped up, yawning loudly. "Because I'm getting tired."

"We'll be there in just a few minutes," Rachael assured her. "As soon as we hit the clearing, my grandmother's house is just to the left."

"We're not really going to *hit* the clearing, are we?" Nicky gulped, holding on even tighter.

"I hope not," Rachael shot back.

Just then, something crackled inside the transport.

"Attention, all units." A voice came from the transmitter on the coppers' control panel. "Be on the lookout for two aliens in a stolen vehicle."

Rachael and Nicky exchanged worried looks.

"Repeat," the voice crackled again. "Be on the lookout

for two aliens who have apparently kidnapped one of our own. They were last seen speeding through zone three in a stolen blue-and-white. Approach with caution. These aliens are believed to be dangerous. If spotted, shoot on sight. Repeat. Shoot the aliens on sight."

"Don't worry," Rachael said. Nicky could tell she was trying to calm him down, but it wasn't working. "My grandmother's house is just around this bend. I promise, she'll get us out of this mess. Grandma always knows what to do."

At Rachael's words, Nicky felt himself relax a little. His grandmother always knew how to make things better too. Maybe Rachael's grandmother could actually help them find a way out of this mess—and find his parents too.

Nicky was starting to feel hopeful—until he caught sight of the landing strip in front of Grandma's house. It was lined with transports that made the sixteen-wheeler look like a toy. These chunks of steel were twice the size of the big rig on the freeway, with too many wheels to count.

Anger surged through Nicky as he stared at Rachael in disbelief. Grandma knew what to do all right—call in the militia!

CHAPTER

19

"You lied!" Nicky cried as the blue-and-white was quickly surrounded by military attack vehicles. Tunnel-like tubes shot out from the transports' thick armored sides. They moved up and down, as if they were seeking a target. "Your grandmother really is the brains behind this operation—isn't she?"

Rachael didn't say a word.

Nicky turned back to the transports, sure that the tunnel-like tubes were some kind of rocket launchers. Manning them were probably dozens of aliens, just waiting to blow Nicky and Zoe away.

In the airspace above, six alien flying machines hovered in place, their sharp chopping blades spinning furiously.

Nicky looked back at Zoe. A lump rose in his throat. He

wanted to say good-bye. He wanted to tell her that even though she was a pain in the butt, she was still his sister, and he really did love her.

But Zoe wasn't even conscious anymore. She'd actually fallen asleep.

Nicky decided it was better to leave her that way. Why wake her up to scare her to death? he reasoned.

But he definitely had some parting words for Rachael.

"I can't believe you did this to us!" he screamed at her. "Why didn't you just let Ickle cut out my brain—it would have been a lot kinder!"

"I'm telling you, Nicky," Rachael replied. "My grandmother didn't do this! She wouldn't hurt an amoeba. And neither would I. What do I have to do to get it through your head? I'M TRYING TO HELP YOU!"

Nicky covered his ears. Rachael's voice was taking on Zoe proportions.

"Attention!" another voice boomed. It rose from the ground, echoing for miles around. "Surrender now," it ordered, "and no one will get hurt."

"What should I do?" Rachael asked Nicky in a panic.

Either Rachael was the best alien actress on Planet X, or she really was on Nicky's side. But that didn't mean Grandma was on their side.

"Niiiii-cky!" Rachael was even beginning to whine like Zoe. "What do you want me to do?"

Like they really had a choice.

"Dock this sucker," Nicky yelped. "Before they blow us to pieces!"

"Where should I put it?" she cried.

"I don't know!" Nicky shot back. "Put it right there!" He pointed to the only clear terrain.

"My grandmother will kill us!" Rachael moaned. "We'll smush all her plants. That's her front lawn!"

"Who cares!" Nicky said, sure that Grandma was going to kill him anyway. "Just do it!" he shouted.

"Okay, okay," Rachael finally agreed. She maneuvered the blue-and-white transport through a row of green tanks and stopped on a brown patch—the center of Grandma's "front lawn."

"Maybe we could make a run for it," Nicky suggested hopelessly.

"We could try." Rachael sounded just as desperate as she reached over the seat to grab Zoe.

But just as Nicky was about to open his hatch, something attached itself to both sides of their transport.

"Gross!" Nicky said. He couldn't tear his eyes away from the terrifying sight. The thing looked like a squiggly brown intestine with pulsating veins. As it wrapped itself around the stolen police transport, it appeared ready to suction off both of the hatches.

"Aaaaaaaaaaaaagghhhhh!" Nicky screamed, squirming away from the hatch. "What the heck is that thing?"

"Aaaaaaaaaaaaagghhhhh!" Rachael screamed too. "I don't know!"

Zoe woke up and immediately joined in the hysterics as well, an entire decibel level above them.

"AAAAAAAGGGGGHHHHH!" she wailed at the top of her lungs. "THERE'S A GIANT WORM SUCKING AT US!"

Just then, Nicky caught sight of something moving through the bizarre tube. *This can't be happening,* he thought. He blinked, hoping he was dreaming. But when he opened his eyes, he saw that it was true.

Ickle the Iceman was coming toward him, with Fat Neck and Skinny two steps behind.

CHAPTER 20

Nicky watched in horror as Dr. Ickle pressed his disgusting face against the smoky gray glass on Nicky's side of the blue-and-white transport. Behind him, Fat Neck and Skinny stood with what looked like scuba diving tanks strapped to their backs. Attached to the tanks were long rubber hoses with some kind of firing device secured on their ends.

Behind Fat Neck and Skinny, two dozen armed aliens marched through the pulsating tube.

Two dozen more militia mutants moved through the tunnel on Rachael's side of the transport.

They were such a terrifying sight, even Zoe was shocked into silence.

"I was wrong about you," Ickle sneered as the fumes from his nose holes steamed up the glass. "You're *not* a clever alien, are you? If you were, you never would have trusted a twelve-year-old girl from another planet, now would you?" He shot Rachael an icy-cold stare. "It was so good of you to bring these aliens back to me, Rachael," he said. "In fact, your grandmother and I have been awaiting your arrival all evening."

Nicky gave her a suspicious look.

"Don't listen to him, Nicky," Rachael cried. "He's the one who's lying! I never would have brought you here if I thought Uncle Ickle and the militia were waiting." She reached out to touch Nicky's arm. "You've got to believe me!"

Ickle smiled smugly as Nicky recoiled from Rachael's touch.

"He's a subspecies, Rachael," Ickle sighed. "I would hardly worry about hurting his feelings. He doesn't have any."

"That's not true!" Rachael shouted at Ickle. "Nicky's my friend. And Zoe's like a sister to me."

"Spare me the theatrics," Ickle groaned. "I haven't the time. Now, you can either abandon this transport voluntarily, or you'll be removed in the same way as your *friends*, which I assure you won't be very pleasant."

Nicky stared at her, waiting for Rachael to finally end the charade and get out of the transport, the easy way.

Ickle was right about my not being clever, he thought. *I've acted like a complete dork.*

But Ickle was wrong about Nicky's feelings. Thanks to Rachael, he'd never felt so crushed or betrayed in his life.

"Come along, my dear," Ickle repeated.

But Rachael didn't budge. "I'm staying with my friends," she shouted defiantly. "You'll have to remove me the same way you're planning to remove Nicky and Zoe!"

"Oh my gosh!" Nicky couldn't believe it. Rachael really had been telling the truth. For a split second, Nicky was actually grateful he was trapped on Planet X, because Rachael was truly turning out to be his very best friend.

"Fine," Ickle growled. "Then it's lights out for everyone!"

Before Nicky could even try to say good-bye, Ickle gave the order: "Fire!"

CHAPTER 21

The aliens in the tubes covered their faces with black rubber masks as Fat Neck and Skinny discharged their weapons.

Within seconds, a hissing sound filled the tube.

Nicky braced himself against the back of his seat, waiting for the deadly rays from the aliens' weapons to sear his flesh.

But the only thing that cut through the transport was a thick, heavy mist.

Clouds of white smoke poured through the seams of the blue-and-white's hatches—just as it had poured through the cracks of Mr. Gogol's plane shortly after Nicky and his family were sucked into the alien spacecraft.

Ickle's not planning to kill us now, Nicky realized. *He's just knocking us out, so he can kill us later!*

Nicky's nostrils started to burn.

"Hold your breath!" he tried to warn Zoe and Rachael. "This is some kind of gas!"

But Nicky's warning came too late.

Rachael looked woozy. And Zoe was already limp.

Nicky covered his face with his hand, trying desperately to function on the tiny bit of air left in his lungs. But Dr. Ickle was watching him. Nicky dropped his hand from his face, held his breath, and pretended to pass out.

Almost immediately, the militia slid open the hatches.

"Take them directly to the EMS transport," Ickle ordered as Fat Neck and Skinny finally stopped firing their weapons.

Nicky opened his left eye a crack. Militia members were lifting Zoe and Rachael from the blue-and-white. They laid them down on the same kind of rubber band and match sticks he'd seen on the news, then carried them off through the tube.

A moment later, Fat Neck and Skinny were reaching for Nicky.

Nicky didn't have to pretend to be limp. Enough gas had gotten into his system to attack all his muscles. He had no control of his limbs.

That was a good thing, because Fat Neck and Skinny had no idea Nicky was still awake.

But Nicky's lungs were starting to burn. If he didn't take a breath soon, they were sure to explode.

As soon as Fat Neck and Skinny laid him down on the

giant rubber band, they picked up the sticks and carried him through the tube as well.

Nicky struggled against the inevitable unconsciousness. He wanted to see where the tube would lead.

Where the heck were they taking him?

The tube led to the "EMS," another strange vehicle equipped with the same kind of beeping machines Ickle had had in his lab.

Nicky caught only a quick glimpse of the place before his lungs forced him to take a deep breath.

A moment later, everything went black.

CHAPTER 22

Unfortunately, it didn't stay black for long.

"Well, well, well." Ickle's foul breath hit Nicky's face the moment he opened his eyes. "Are we ready for our alien autopsy?"

Autopsy? What was this maniac planning now? Nicky wasn't dead!

Hey! Nicky wanted to scream. *What happened to just cutting my brain out?*

But Nicky's tongue felt swollen again. And his mouth was too dry to speak.

"Now, this is going to be fun," Ickle informed him.

Nicky's eyes scanned the walls around him. He was no longer in the EMS transport. He was in a room he didn't recognize.

"Where am I?" Nicky finally choked out the words.

"You're in a government-secured, secret facility," Ickle informed him. "Thanks to your exploits, and WPX news, we felt it would be safer to move you to a location where no one on the planet could possibly find you."

"Safer for who?" Nicky blurted out nervously as he caught sight of the iron clamps around his ankles and arms.

Ickle snorted again. "Safer for all of us, of course."

"And where are my parents and Zoe?" Nicky asked.

"Secured," Ickle answered.

"And Rachael?"

"*She's* being punished as we speak," Ickle said. "It's time for us to stop these pleasantries and get down to business: your autopsy."

"And what's that?" Nicky hoped that the word "autopsy" would mean something different in alien. It did—and it didn't.

"An autopsy is the procedure by which a scientist like myself cuts open a living organism to study its innards," Ickle informed him.

"Excuse me," Nicky started, "but aren't I supposed to be a goner first?"

"If you're lucky," Ickle shot back. "But you're not very lucky, are you? If you were, you wouldn't be clamped to this operating table, now would you?"

"What kind of cruel planet is this?" Nicky demanded. He was starting to get as angry as he was scared. "On my planet, nobody does an autopsy on a living being! Don't you aliens have any respect for life?"

"Aliens?" Ickle snorted again. "You're calling *me* an alien? You really are a brazen little bugger, aren't you?"

Just then another alien stepped into the room through a swinging steel door.

"I've been sent to assist you," it said as it headed for Ickle, pushing a silver tray on wheels.

Nicky turned to look, but he couldn't see much of the new alien's face. It was wrapped with some kind of puke-colored mask, and a cap covered the alien's head. Still, Nicky was pretty sure this one was female. Aside from the high pitch of the alien's voice, she was wearing the same kind of silver clumps below her ear holes that Rachael wore. And her eyes were as blue as Rachael's too.

"Where are my usual assistants?" Ickle wanted to know.

"They called in sick," the alien in the mask answered. "So I'm filling in."

"Well, I hope you know what you're doing," Ickle huffed.

"Absolutely," the alien in the mask answered. "I know exactly what I'm doing." She looked straight at Nicky. Then the crinkly skin above her left eye slid downward for a second.

Nicky did a double take. If he didn't know better, he would have thought that the creature had winked at him.

"Did you bring the circular saw?" Ickle asked his new assistant.

"Number one on my checklist," she answered, lifting a

jagged-toothed blade from the table. A black, snakelike cord dangled from the side of the hunk of metal. "Want me to start her up?"

"Please," Ickle answered. "Just make sure that when you open the body, you saw straight up the middle."

"No problémo," the new assistant answered. Then she pulled on the cord and the "circular saw" buzzed to life.

Please don't do it, Nicky thought as the saw came closer.

"Just stay calm, honey," the new assistant told Nicky. The jagged teeth of the saw were only an inch away from his chest. "Believe me—you'll be checking out of here in just a few minutes."

*W*rrrrrrrrrrrrrrrrrr!

The sound of the saw cutting its way through the air was nowhere near as horrible as the screaming that followed.

But the bloodcurdling screams weren't coming from Nicky—they were coming from Ickle!

"WHOOOOOOAAAAAAAA DOGGGGGGGGIEEEEE!" Ickle's alien lungs let loose as his new assistant suddenly turned the saw toward *his* chest.

"I'm no doggie!" the new assistant shouted. "Now stand back, you nincompoop!" she ordered, swinging the saw in front of him wildly.

"What do you think you're doing?" Ickle yelped.

"A good deed," his assistant answered. Then she pulled the mask from her face and flashed a big alien smile at Ickle.

"Mom!" The bottom half of Ickle's mouth fell off its hinges. "How on earth did you get in here?"

"On my broomstick," the old lady shot back.

Nicky blinked hard. This was Ickle's mother?

"Well, you're just going to have to leave," Ickle informed her.

"Oh, I'm leaving all right," she said. "But I'm taking him with me." She pointed at Nicky.

Nicky only hoped she was planning to "take him" all in one piece.

"Are you out of your mind?" Ickle snapped. "You can't interfere with the interest of science!"

"I'm your mother," the old lady barked. "I can interfere with anything I want! Besides, you're the one who's out of his mind. I knew it when you were just an egg. Why do you think I loved your brother best?"

"You only loved Sonny because he gave you a grand-daughter!" Ickle huffed.

That line hit Nicky like a ton of bricks.

This wasn't just Ickle's mother! This was Rachael's grandmother!

"Don't be ridiculous," the old lady snorted. "I loved Sonny best because Sonny had a heart. Rachael was an unexpected blessing. You, on the other hand, have always been a curse. You're a cold-blooded, status-seeking yo-yo! I still can't believe you came from my gene pool."

"You'll never get away with this," Ickle whined.

"Oh, no?" She grinned. "Just watch me. There's no way

in the universe I'm going to let you harm one of my inter-galactic friends."

"You really do belong with the noo-noos," Ickle grumbled. "And these aliens!"

"Alien-shmalien," his mother sneered. "We're all the same on the inside."

With the circular saw still spinning at Ickle, the old lady hit a switch on the wall. Suddenly the iron clamps around Nicky's limbs were released.

"There you go, junior," she told Nicky. "Now let's get a move on it, shall we?"

"My name's Nicky," he informed her as he sprang from the table. "And you're Rachael's grandmother, right?"

"That's right," she said. "But you can call me Grandma."

"Okay," Nicky agreed. "But listen, Grandma, I can't leave here without my mom and dad and my little sister, Zoe."

"I know that, sweetie," Grandma said. "They're already safely secured—in the back of my new set of wheels. Rachael's there too."

"You mean they've already escaped?" Nicky asked.

"Yup," she said. "When Grandma sets her mind to something, rest assured it gets done. Now put on these scrubs." She tossed Nicky a bundle of alien clothes she pulled from under the silver table. "And you," she told Ickle, "lie down on this bed."

"Don't do this, Ma," Ickle pleaded. "You're only asking for trouble. If these aliens don't eat you or something, the government will."

"That's if they catch me," Grandma said. "And with the way I fly, that's not going to happen. Now lie down on that bed!"

She aimed the saw at Ickle's butt, which forced him to do as she ordered.

The moment he was down, she hit the switch that locked the clamps around his limbs.

"*Hasta la vista*, baby!" She laughed, turning off the circular saw. "That's a foreign language, you know," she told Nicky.

"Yes," Nicky said, pulling up his alien pants. "I know."

Grandma grabbed Nicky's hand and led him toward the door.

"Now just stay close," she told him. "And act like a nincompoop. That way we'll blend."

"Okay," Nicky said, following Grandma's lead.

Acting like a nincompoop was definitely the ticket. Nicky and Grandma made their way through the halls of the government facility in no time at all.

There was only one problem.

"We're stealing a government transport?" Nicky yelped when he saw Grandma's new wheels. The coppers' blue-and-white had been bad enough. But this EMS transport was bound to attract all kinds of attention.

"Just climb on in and let me worry about that," Grandma said. "Besides, don't you want to see your mom and your dad?"

Nicky's heart suddenly lightened. He was dying to see his parents!

But when he climbed aboard, his elation turned to horror. Mr. and Mrs. Gogol were lying flat on their backs, strapped to two rolling slabs. Neither of them was awake. And neither of them seemed to be breathing.

Rachael was standing over Mrs. Gogol, pressing a tiny black cup to her heart. The cup was attached to two long tubes that stuck out of Rachael's ear holes.

Zoe was curled up in the corner of the transport, snoring up a storm.

"What happened to them?" Nicky's heart was about to climb out of his chest without the help of an autopsy. "Are they . . ."

He couldn't even say the word.

"No," Rachael assured him. "They're both still breathing. You see?" She took Nicky's hand and laid it on Mrs. Gogol's stomach.

Nicky felt the up and down movement, then sighed his relief.

Rachael did the same with his father.

"But then why are they unconscious?" he asked.

"They must still be under the gas," Rachael said. "Their heartbeats are strong. I'm sure they're going to be fine."

Just then, Grandma gasped loudly. "Uh-oh! Looks like we've already got company!"

Nicky looked out through the hatch. Fat Neck and Skinny were racing toward them, followed by a bunch of government goons.

"Take off, Grandma!" Rachael shouted.

"Okie-dokie," Grandma said, revving her engines. "Hang on to your hats!"

Grandma tore off so quickly, Nicky couldn't hang on to a thing.

Boy, Nicky thought as the centrifugal force practically peeled his face off, *Grandma wasn't kidding when she said no one could catch her.*

But where were they going?

Rachael was thinking the very same thing.

"Hey, Grandma," she called out. "Where are you headed?"

"To the airfield," Grandma announced. "I have a hunch about something."

"What's that mean?" Nicky asked Rachael.

"I don't know," Rachael told him. "But when Grandma has a hunch, something big always happens."

"Something good big or something bad big?" Nicky wanted to know.

But Rachael didn't have a chance to answer. Suddenly, something *really* big was hovering above them.

The airspace rumbled like thunder as the EMS transport started to shake.

"What's going on?" Rachael shrieked.

"I don't know!" Nicky shouted back.

"Jumping Jehoshaphat!" Grandma exclaimed. "I knew I felt something electric in the air!"

Electric wasn't the proper term for it. *Flying saucer* was!

Nicky couldn't believe his eyes as he stared up at the huge, swirling dish.

"Oh, no," Nicky cried. "Here we go again!"

For a moment, he was sure they were in for another harrowing alien adventure. Until a blinding white light shot down from the saucer and beamed them aboard the spaceship called *Xorg*.

CHAPTER 24

Nicky felt as if every molecule in his body was blasting apart before the huge beam of light finally dropped them off—all in one piece—in the belly of a familiar transport.

Rachael was trembling as she checked out her hands and her legs to make sure they were all still intact.

"Geez, oh, man," she murmured. "It felt like my whole body was disintegrating."

"It was," Nicky told her. "That's how this saucer beamed us aboard."

"You're kidding me!" Rachael gasped.

Nicky shook his head. "Hasn't this ever happened to you before?" he asked.

"No!" Rachael told him. "This is totally alien to me."

"Not to me," Nicky replied, smiling. "But it's pretty cool, isn't it?"

Just then, Grandma let out a *yahoo!* "Wow," she exclaimed. "That was some ride!"

Nicky was about to agree when a familiar voice called out his name, in his own language.

"Nicolai?"

"Dad!" Nicky cried. "You're okay!" He threw his arms around his father.

"I'm fine," Mr. Gogol assured him as Mrs. Gogol rose to her feet.

Neither one of them looked very pleased to see Rachael and Grandma.

"Stay back," Mr. Gogol warned in the aliens' language, pointing his finger as if it were some kind of weapon.

"It's okay, Dad." Nicky jumped in front of him. "These are my friends. That's Rachael." He gestured toward her first. "And that's Rachael's grandmother. But we can call her Grandma."

"Howdie-doo." Grandma smiled.

Mr. Gogol shot Nicky a disapproving look. "None of these aliens are our friends," he told Nicky.

"These two are, Dad," Nicky insisted. "They saved our lives. And they risked their own lives to do it. Grandma's the one who got you and Mom away from Dr. Ickle. And Rachael's been helping me and Zoe from the start."

"Speaking of Zoe . . ." Mrs. Gogol said. She looked around groggily. "Where is she?"

"I'm right here, Mommy!" Zoe squealed in delight. Her eyes had popped wide open the moment she heard

Mrs. Gogol's voice. She leaped to her feet and jumped into her mother's arms.

"Oh, my baby!" Mrs. Gogol kissed Zoe. "Are you okay?"

"I'm fine, Mommy," Zoe answered. "Thanks to Rachael and Grandma. They saved us from Ickle the Iceman!"

At that Mrs. Gogol turned to face Rachael and Grandma. "I'm eternally grateful to you for taking care of my children."

"*No problémo*," Grandma told her. "They're just like my own. Well, just like my Rachael, anyway," she corrected herself.

"Where are we?" Mr. Gogol asked, looking disoriented.

But Nicky didn't have a chance to answer before the walls of their transport disintegrated around them.

Rachael's eyes grew wide. "Holy smokes," she exclaimed. "This thing looks just like the spaceship in *Star Trek*!"

"Yeah," Grandma agreed. "But the crew members are green!"

Rachael and Grandma looked frightened.

But Mr. Gogol heaved a huge sigh of relief as he spotted the bloated green heads with the wide brown eyes staring back at them. "They heard us," he said, smiling at Mrs. Gogol. "The *Xorg* actually got our signal."

"You sent them a signal?" Nicky asked.

"Yes," Mr. Gogol answered. "Just before the alien craft sucked us aboard and gassed us. Captain Zenex must have picked up the signal, then followed us here with the *Xorg*."

Just then Captain Zenex himself appeared. He bowed

his head and touched his antennae with each of the Gogols'. That was the usual greeting on Nicky's planet.

"I trust you are all well." Captain Zenex spoke in Nicky's native tongue.

"Thanks to you and your capable crew," Mr. Gogol replied.

"And Grandma and Rachael!" Nicky jumped in.

"Yes." Mrs. Gogol echoed the thought. "Those two female aliens have acted as allies," she told the captain.

Captain Zenex and his crew slowly approached Rachael and Grandma. The two of them looked ready to pass out, especially when the captain and his men started to chatter to one another and scan Rachael's head with the glowing tips of their fingers.

"It's okay, Rachael," Nicky assured her. "They're just trying to get to know you."

"Well, what are they saying?" Rachael gulped.

Just then, Rachael got her answer, directly from the captain.

"I'm sorry." He apologized to Rachael and Grandma in their language. "It's rude of me to speak in my native tongue."

"Don't worry about it," Grandma told him. "We can learn to speak whatever language you want."

The captain smiled. "Fortunately, you won't have to concern yourselves with that." He turned toward Mr. Gogol. "Allies or not, they'll have to go back."

"Why?" Nicky cried. "These are my friends!"

"We don't want to go back!" Rachael chimed in. "Nicky and I made a deal!"

"Yes, I know," Captain Zenex told her. "I read your mind. You no longer have your mother and father so you are forced to live with your evil uncle, Ickle. He makes you go to the Vroom School, which is like a prison camp. You were hoping Nicky could take you away from all that."

"That's right!" Rachael was amazed.

"And because of some legal complications, you're not allowed to live with your grandmother. So she's forced to live all by herself out in a desert, and everyone thinks she belongs with the noo-noos."

"You got that right," Grandma said.

"So why can't they stay?" Nicky wanted to know.

"This is a complicated matter," Captain Zenex told Nicky. "I was given strict orders by Cranium Command that once the rescue was complete, I was to destroy Planet X, or Earth, as these aliens call it. After carefully studying the inhabitants these past few days, Cranium Command has come to the conclusion that Earthlings have no redeeming qualities at all."

"What?" Nicky's heart started to pound.

"They're violent, irrational, superstitious, and destructive," Captain Zenex went on. "They are a danger to our solar system."

"That's not true," Nicky blurted out. "Not all of the aliens are like that. Look at Grandma and Rachael."

"Two aliens hardly build a strong case for total tolerance, Nicolai," Captain Zenex pointed out.

"Okay . . ." Nicky said, racking his brains to come up with another example. "There was an alien truck driver too," he told the captain. "*I* crashed into *him,* and *he* was worried about *me.*"

"Did he know you were different?" Captain Zenex asked.

"Well, no," Nicky answered.

The captain scowled.

"But Rachael and Grandma can't be the only good aliens on the planet!" Nicky continued to defend his beliefs.

Captain Zenex didn't answer. Instead, he pulled Mr. Gogol and some of his senior officers aside. Then he radioed in to Cranium Command.

Nicky couldn't hear what was being said. But when Captain Zenex finally broke the connection, they all nodded in agreement and headed back toward Nicky.

"We've made a decision," the captain said. "Your friends can stay with us, Nicolai, as long as they don't behave like all those other Earthlings."

"You've got my word, Captain." Nicky smiled as he gave Rachael the thumbs-up. "These aliens will not behave like aliens."

"I certainly hope so," Zenex said.

"What about Planet X?" Nicky asked nervously.

"I've been given my orders," the captain answered. He moved toward the "HOT" button in the center of the *Xorg* control panel and lifted his glowing green finger over it. "Sorry, Nicolai," he said, shooting a look over his shoulder. "But that whole stinking planet is toast!"

Get ready for more . . .

*Here's a preview of the next spine-chilling book
from A. G. Cascone*

WELCOME TO THE TERROR-GO-ROUND

*When Alex and Joey sneak out in the middle of the night
to check out the strange carnival that's just rolled into
town, they soon discover that the rides are a scream . . .
and the games are to die for.*

As Alex and Joey stepped up to the Terror-Go-Round,
the ride came to a sudden stop.

"How did that happen?" Joey asked.

"I don't know," Alex said. "It stopped all by itself." Alex
was getting more freaked out by the minute. This whole
carnival seemed very strange.

"Maybe it's on a timer," Joey suggested. "Let's get on
and see if it starts back up again."

"Why do you want to ride a stupid merry-go-round?" Alex asked, trying to sound indifferent. The truth was, *he* didn't want to ride it.

"Because it's not a merry-go-round," Joey said, smiling mischievously. "It's the Terror-Go-Round. And it says, 'Ride if you dare.' You know I can't pass up a dare." With that, Joey hopped aboard and started checking out the horses. He climbed on the meanest-looking one of all. "Get on," he told Alex.

"Forget it," Alex shot back.

"What are you, chicken?" Joey taunted.

"No," Alex said, not even convincing himself. "I just think it's stupid, that's all."

"Bawk-bawk-bawk, bawk-bawk," Joey clucked at him.

That did it. There was no way Alex could let Joey make fun of him. His sense of honor overshadowed his good judgment, and he stepped onto the ride to prove he was no coward.

"There," he said to Joey. "Are you happy now?"

"Not until you get on a horse," Joey said, reaching over to pat the one next to him.

Without another word, Alex slid his foot into the metal stirrup and lifted himself into the saddle.

"Now what?" Alex asked. "Are we just going to sit here like a couple of jerks, hoping the ride starts up again?"

"Give it a minute," Joey answered.

They waited a minute. Then two. Then three.

"See," Alex said. "Nothing's happening."

"There's got to be a way to start this thing," Joey

insisted, climbing down from his horse. "I'll bet there's a switch somewhere."

As Joey began inspecting the mirrored walls at the center of the ride, Alex climbed off his own horse to follow.

"Here we go," Joey called from the other side of the ride.

Set into the walls was a glass booth with a mechanical ticket-taker inside—a man-size dummy wearing a tuxedo and a top hat. Behind him was a blinking sign that read "1997."

The dummy's wooden mouth snapped open. "Tickets, please," he said as Joey stepped up to his window.

Joey dug into his pocket and shuffled through his tickets. He pulled two out of the stack. "Free ride on the Terror-Go-Round—one way,'" he read aloud before placing them into the dummy's outstretched hand.

The dummy's fingers curled tightly around the tickets as he pulled his hand away. Then he began to laugh maniacally.

The ride did not move.

But the wooden horses did! They all began neighing wildly. Their heads moved up and down, and their hooves pawed at the ground.

"This is too cool!" Joey exclaimed.

But Alex didn't think it was cool at all. In fact, he thought it was scary. He was just about to jump off the ride when it began to spin.

Joey leaped onto the painted horse nearest him.

The horse reared up onto its hind legs, and Joey threw his arms around its neck, holding on for dear life. "This is great!" he shouted to Alex as the mechanical horse continued to buck up and down like a bronco.

Alex wasn't about to get on one of those horses. But as he backed away, the horse behind him wedged its head between Alex's legs and flung him up into the saddle.

Now Alex was the one holding on for dear life. He screamed his head off as the horse galloped beneath him and the ride began to spin faster and faster. If the horse didn't toss him, he was sure the centrifugal force would.

They were moving so quickly that everything outside the ride became one big blur.

Alex was sure he was going to throw up. "How do we stop this thing?" he cried.

"Stop it?" Joey laughed. "I hope it goes on forever. This is even better than a roller coaster."

But the ride didn't go on forever. After just a few minutes of bumping and spinning, the Terror-Go-Round jerked to a halt.

Alex heaved a sigh of relief as he lowered his head and closed his eyes. He was shaking so badly, he knew his legs wouldn't hold him if he tried to climb off the horse. Besides that, his stomach was still in his throat, and he was afraid any movement would only bring it the rest of the way up.

"Alex," Joey said in a quavering voice.

Alex didn't answer. He couldn't.

"Uh, Alex." Joey's voice sounded even more shaky. "Something really weird has happened."

Slowly, Alex raised his head and opened his eyes. He immediately saw the source of Joey's concern.

He squeezed his eyes shut again.

This can't be, he told himself. *It's impossible.*

But when he opened his eyes again, the problem was still there.

It wasn't nighttime anymore. It was the middle of the day. And the carnival was teeming with people—strange-looking people, people who seemed to be from another world.

About the Author

A. G. Cascone is the pseudonym of two authors who happen to be sisters . . . "The Twisted Sisters." In addition to *Deadtime Stories*, they have written six books, two horror-movie screenplays, and several pop songs, including one top-ten hit.

If you want to find out more about DEADTIME STORIES or A. G. Cascone, look on the World Wide Web at: http://www.bookwire.com/titles/deadtime/

Also, we'd love to hear from you! You can write to:
A. G. Cascone
c/o Troll
100 Corporate Drive
Mahwah, NJ 07430

Or you can send e-mail directly to:
agcascone@bookwire.com

Read all of the silly, spooky, cool, and creepy

$3.50 each

*Available at your favorite bookstore . . .
or use this form to order by mail.*

Please send me the books I have checked above. I am enclosing $_____ (please add $2.00 for shipping and handling). Send check or money order payable to Troll Communications — no cash or C.O.D.s, please — to Troll Communications, Customer Service, 2 Lethbridge Plaza, Mahwah, NJ 07430.

Name _____

Address_____

City _____State_____ZIP _____

Age _____   Where did you buy this book? _____

Please allow approximately four weeks for delivery. Offer good in the U.S. only. Sorry, mail orders are not available to residents of Canada. Price subject to change.